D1375827

BS

Please renew or return items by the date shown on your receipt

www.hertfordshire.gov.uk/libraries

Renewals and enquiries: 0300 123 4049

Textphone for hearing or 0300 123 4041
speech impaired users:

11.16

Hertfordshire

525 757 05 1

BY GAIL CARRIGER

POISON
OR
PROTECT

A DELIGHTFULLY DEADLY NOVELLA

GAIL CARRIGER

GAIL CARRIGER LLC

GAIL CARRIGER, LLC

Cover photo © Perry Gallagher. All rights reserved.
Corset by Dark Garden Corsetry & Couture
Cover © 2016 by Gail Carriger, LLC, assembled by Starla Huchton
Formatting by Nina Pierce of Seaside Publications

ISBN 978-1-944751-05-0

*For every one of my fans who reached out and said,
"If Gail Carriger writes it, I will read it."
I've written it.
Now it's up to you.*

CHAPTER ONE

The Game Begins

March 1867, on a train platform…

Gavin knew who she was the moment he saw her. He also knew there was a good chance he would have to kill her. Assuming, of course, she didn't kill him first.

Lady Preshea Villentia. The Mourning Star. Widowed too many times under suspicious circumstances, too smart to be caught, and too beautiful to be ostracized. She was like opiates – expensive, intoxicating, and deadly in large doses.

He wasn't sure *exactly* how he knew it was Lady Villentia. They'd never been introduced. They didn't attend the same social functions (her circles being more rarefied than those of a mere army captain).

Also, she was standing with her back to him.

Yet he did know her.

He'd read the papers and dismissed their breathless descriptions as romanticized nonsense. He'd seen the sketches and assumed a great deal of artistic license. To his chagrin, he realized now that neither had done her justice.

She moved into profile.

The lady was a porcelain doll, perfect in every detail, delicate as fine china and no doubt more costly. Yet she directed the porters with the sure command of any field marshal.

She must be attending the same house party. There was no other reason for a woman of such exalted skills to disembark at a country station. It was reasonable to assume her ultimate destination was the Snodgrove gathering. And equally reasonable to assume, Lady Villentia being an assassin, that she was there to kill the duke. Which meant Gavin was there to stop her.

She turned into the light.

It wasn't that a chorus of angels opened up and sang. Nor did pixies sprinkle fairy dust in his vision. For the day was all gloom and grey, and the engine of the train was as smelly and loud as may be. Gavin, however, was horrified to feel his world start to shift, right under his massive boots. Usually, he was brick-wall steady, and brick-wall solid. But now his entire body, like a magnet to iron, centered on Lady Villentia.

Lust, is it? Isna that convenient? Hell's waistcoat.

Her figure was neat and slender under a green carriage dress of pure simplicity with gleaming jet buttons down the front. She wore a little velvet hat, as dark and glossy as her hair. She lifted one hand to test its presence, showing black leather gloves.

"My, my, that one has stepped off the pages of a French fashion periodical." Jack followed Gavin's gaze and was struck as well, although perhaps not quite so dumbstruck.

"Nay. Too wee for that," Gavin was moved to grumble.

Jack laughed, a spark of joy that caught the lady's attention. Fortunately, Jack then lowered his voice. "Yes, yes, you like more to grab hold of."

Gavin was known amongst his friends for his abhorrence of tiny females. But such a widely stated preference suddenly seemed absurd.

Every part of Lady Villentia was covered but for her heart-shaped face – white and emotionless. A ceramic doll in truth and likely just as cold. Except there… For one unguarded moment beneath all that beauty, her eyes flashed a depth of misery he'd seen only in the worst slums.

She blinked and it was gone.

Jack continued, "That one looks more wax than human. Were it not daylight, I'd think her vampire."

Gavin did not point out the idiocy of that statement. Even were it night, no female vampire traveled. Queens could not leave their hives. He had to presume Jack knew this, or his friend was thicker than treacle.

Luggage accumulated, they all moved towards the exit. Yet they were a thousand miles apart for lack of introduction.

Lady Villentia even walked beautifully. Gavin found himself, preferences be damned, imagining what it might like to unbutton that dress. One jet bead at a time, from top to bottom, until he knelt at those tiny feet.

Are ye daft? he reprimanded himself. *Assassin?*

A private dirigible awaited them outside the station. The Duke of Snodgrove, a consummate host, had seen fit to provide the most modern conveyance. Gavin could have wished him to perdition. He detested floating, and had hoped for something faster after so long a train ride. Dirigibles were all well and good if one wanted to waft about the countryside, taking in views. Gavin wanted his tea.

And not to have to kill Lady Villentia.

But tea first.

The lady in question regarded the Snodgrove crest with her head cocked, showing a slender white neck.

At their approach, she turned with a practiced smile. "I believe we may be traveling together, gentlemen. To Bickerstung Manor?"

Gavin and Jack responded as expected, with bows of agreement. Gavin thought her smile slightly painful, both for her to give and for him to receive. The sorrow in it hurt the space between his eyes. *Verra inconvenient.*

The jet buttons winked at him.

It was for her to continue. "Might we dispense with the formalities? Otherwise, it will make for an awkward float. I believe our host is under the mistaken impression that we are already acquainted." She spoke with such precision. Her pert lips slaughtered each word as it left her mouth.

Gavin recovered his voice. "Oh, aye? And why is

that, lass?"

"I believe he thinks *everyone* knows me."

At which juncture Jack, the nincompoop, blurted, "Good God, you're the Mourning Star, aren't you?"

Preshea refused to hope that her target was the larger gentleman. He looked like some minor Greek god, all rock-hewn inertia. Admittedly, since it was drizzling, a damp god.

Yet she *had* hoped. When he spoke and his accent proved to be nested firmly in the Highlands, a part of her was crushed with disappointment. This was not her target. This was the target's inconvenient Scottish friend.

Which meant she must focus on the other man, the lanky one with the foolish smile. *Pity* – she gave a small sigh – *I'd have enjoyed climbing Mount Olympus.*

Olympus winced when his friend titled her with that ridiculous moniker. *Sensitive mountain.*

She issued a tinkling laugh, not too brittle, just enough to subtly hint that she was hurt but not angered – playing upon sympathies.

"Jack, dinna be an idiot," barked the Scotsman.

Preshea assessed him from under her lashes. He held himself like a soldier, with the confidence of a man who has nothing to gain or lose in any given social situation. He was, without doubt, a danger to her schemes.

"Pray do not concern yourselves. I'm aware of

the regretful stylings of the popular press." In point of fact, Preshea was proud of Mourning Star. It had taken two dead husbands before they called her anything special at all, and when it stuck through the next two, she knew herself to be infamous. It could have been worse; some of her American counterparts got monikers like Black Widow. *Absolutely ghastly.*

The Scotsman gave his companion another quelling look and then doffed his hat. "Captain Ruthven, at your service, Lady Villentia." His hair was brown. However, dry and in the sunlight, it might be flecked with gold. He gestured with one massive hand. "This feckless blighter is Mr Jackson."

Preshea bowed her head graciously. "Captain Ruthven, Mr Jackson, delighted. Shall we get on? If we make good time, we may arrive before tea. Captain, if you wouldn't mind, my bags?"

The Scotsman gave her a measured look. She widened her eyes, keeping them soft and limpid, knowing that even the best of men were prone to sink into them. He did not succumb, did not even look dazed, only inclined his head and went to supervise the loading of the luggage.

This, as Preshea intended, ensured that Mr Jackson must assist her into the dirigible and see her settled.

"Traveling without your maid, Lady Villentia?"

"Afraid for your reputation, Mr Jackson? Or mine? How thoughtful. I'm afraid the deed is done. That very reputation ensures I'm rarely impinged upon."

Reminding him of her history might be going a

step too far, but the young man laughed as if she had made a rollicking joke. "I'm not afraid of you."

She smiled then and watched his eyes dilate. *Too easy. Why is it always so easy?* "I should hope not, Mr Jackson. A gentleman like yourself would never be influenced by the base opinions of scandalmongers."

"Exactly so, my lady." He puffed with pride.

"So, shall we be friends?"

Mr Jackson was delighted by this premature offer. "At once!"

The Scotsman joined them. His large frame shook the dirigible, tilting it towards the ground as he hauled himself inside.

"I canna believe this contraption will float with Jack and me weighing it down. Helmsman?"

"No fear, milord." The helmsman was visible out the back window, directing the aircraft. He drew up the mooring rope. They bobbed easily into the air.

Captain Ruthven took great care with his movements. Here was a man accustomed to his size and circumspect about applying it. He would be deadly in a fight when he finally let those coiled muscles free. *Let us hope it never comes to that.* But oh, it would be glorious to see.

He settled, with ill-disguised discomfort, onto the reverse bench next to his friend. Both men were big, although the captain had a good deal more mass than Mr Jackson. The dirigible bench did not easily accommodate the pair.

"Well, then, gentlemen, how do you know our host?"

This pleasant opening set Mr Jackson chattering

– first about the Blingchesters, who would also be in attendance (the Scotsman rolled his eyes and called them "England's foremost cadgers") and then about the reason for his invitation. His ladylove. The woman Preshea had been hired to prevent his marrying.

"And what is her name?" Preshea deployed politeness.

A long pause.

Captain Ruthven grinned. "Dinna say you've forgotten?"

Mr Jackson whacked his friend with a rolled-up newspaper. "I was marshaling my thoughts, the better to do her justice."

"Weel, now you're in for it, Lady Villentia."

"Oh, dear, what have I wrought?"

Mr Jackson found his voice. "Lady Violet is Duke Snodgrove's eldest daughter. She's absolutely topping. A divine mango from heaven. Or do I mean banana from heaven? Well, she's both. An elegant bastion of womanhood."

The flowery turn to his phrasing indicated a worrying degree of affection for the lady. Was it possible that this fortune hunter actually believed himself *in love* with the chit? That would be a complication.

Preshea probed gently. "I myself have never met the lady. She sounds pleasant indeed."

"Prepare to be delighted," promised the lovesick swain.

"Well, if she is so fortunate as to secure your attention, I cannot help but be so."

Mr Jackson chuckled. "I'm known as an *expert*

judge of character."

Captain Ruthven made a pained face.

Preshea was moved to be coy. "The good captain disagrees with this assessment?"

"Jack is pally with everyone."

"Thus making himself agreeable through lack of discretion. You object to this approach?"

"Nay. 'Tis one of his charms. I myself am na one to jump in so."

Jack turned. "And thus you limit your enjoyment."

"You two are unlikely companions." Preshea steered them onto a topic she knew would prove pleasurable and no doubt endear her to both. "How did you meet?"

Mr Jackson jumped on the opening. "We share a club. This may shock you, but I'm as likely as not to get myself in a pickle. I was deep in the soup over a cheese bun. Ruthven rescued me and has continued to do so ever since. Stalwart chap."

"Oh, indeed?" Preshea cast a friendly look at the big Scotsman. Was the captain like this with Mr Jackson alone, or with all his friends? A white knight could sometimes be manipulated to see her as worthy of saving. Although victim was not a role she enjoyed playing.

"It began out o' goodness and has become dire habit," admitted Captain Ruthven. Preshea wondered if he was attending this house party in order to assist with his friend's suit or to persuade him against it. She also wondered if he were prone to airsickness; he was looking peaky.

Mr Jackson nudged the captain in a jolly way, bumping the Scotsman against the side of the cabin.

The two gentlemen were quite squeezed. It was a ridiculous nicety that Preshea should sit alone, when she was half the size of either and not prone to a feeble stomach. Even as she told herself she was not concerned by the captain's pallor, she found herself making an offer.

"Mr Jackson, why not sit next to me? It seems preposterous to insist on etiquette when the two of you are so much more than that bench allows."

"What a kind thought! But poor old Ruthven here is a bad floater – he should sit facing."

Captain Ruthven looked properly horrified. "I couldna possibly."

"Don't be silly. You're positively green, old chap. You know facing will help."

After further protestations, the big Scotsman shifted to sit next to Preshea. Mr Jackson slid over until he was across from her. This allowed both men to stretch their long legs. Preshea was not opposed – it put her face to face with her target. Unfortunately, it also put that mountain of warm muscles intimately close to her. She held herself aloof, noting that the Scotsman attempted to do the same.

He smells like Christmas – fresh pine boughs and spices. What right has a man to smell so good?

Mr Jackson remained endearingly concerned for his friend. "If the lady doesn't mind, I'll pop open the window."

Preshea did not mind. The weather was unpleasant, but she welcomed fresh air. Not for the sake of the dirigible's motion, for she was an excellent floater, having attended a finishing school in the skies. No, she wished to blow away Captain Ruthven's intoxicating scent.

Preshea Buss! she yelled in her own head, using her maiden name, the one that hurt the most. *No living man has ever brought you anything good. They are to be used, not enjoyed. Focus on the target.*

Captain Ruthven recovered a little of his color. "Beg pardon, Lady Villentia. I'm a sorry traveler. I'd sooner ride, but Jack tells me it isna the done thing."

"Gentlemen ride once they are *in* the country, Ruthven, old hat. They do not ride *to* the country."

"Which seems daft." The captain looked to Preshea for support. "Isna the purpose of country life riding?"

Mr Jackson issued a gormless grin. "Yes, but one *gets* there by dirigible. What do you take us for? Barbarians?"

Captain Ruthven's eyes were intent. "Thus I send my lovely Rusticate into Berkshire separately with my batman, and you find me here, crowding lasses in dirigibles. I canna apologize enough."

"My dear sir, you are hardly responsible for your size."

Mr Jackson said, "Ruthven forgets that since he resigned his commission, Mawkins is his *valet*, not his batman."

Preshea had noticed the gaffe.

The Scotsman winced, which could be from the mistake in etiquette, or something more sinister. Was he still in military employ, perhaps in some secret capacity? *Or is my training making me unreasonably suspicious?*

She probed. "You were in the cavalry, then?"

"Nay. Coldsteam Guards. But I'm an admirer of horseflesh."

An Irregular, was he? That meant he would be exceptionally comfortable with the supernatural.

"And you, lass? Do you ride?"

"I can, but not well, I'm ashamed to admit." Preshea was vaguely aware she ought to object to being called *lass*. After all, she had worked hard to become a proper lady. But she rather liked it, especially when delivered in that rumbling burr of his. The voice equivalent of mulled wine, warm and heavily spiced.

She moved quickly on from that thought. "My skill set is in quite the opposite direction. It is unladylike to brag, but I could steer this dirigible, if needed."

Both men looked more admiring than shocked. *Good, I have judged them correctly.* These were that unusual breed of male that admired a capable female.

Preshea found herself in an unexpected predicament. Enjoying the float, fighting an inclination for the wrong man, and having a genuine affection for both. They seemed so very decent. *This is ridiculous. I don't like people. I certainly don't like men!* It was highly inconvenient. However, she would ignore it as she had ignored all such inconveniences over the years.

Gavin watched as the footman handed Lady Villentia down from the dirigible. Jack jumped down after. Gavin followed.

He heard the poor footman whisper under his breath, "Crikey," and gave a tiny nod of sympathy. *I ken how you feel, lad.*

The Duke and Duchess of Snodgrove stood waiting to receive them.

"Welcome. You are the last to arrive." The duke was one of those remarkable politicians who looked exactly like his caricature – tall, stooped, and lined.

"With tea near to serving." His lady wife had an eye to the practicalities. "You are timely." The Duchess of Snodgrove was the opposite of her husband. Her features were delicate and her form well padded. She looked like the human representation of a comfortable settee.

Lady Villentia gave an elegant curtsey of the exact correct depth for a duke and his duchess. Gavin was impressed. He might act and sound provincial (it worked in his favor, to be constantly underestimated), but he'd attended Eton and knew all the forms. Her delivery was perfection itself.

"It is your dirigible that has seen us safely here. Thank you for the kind attention, Your Grace." She slid as smoothly into the role of guest as she had into that of fellow traveler.

Overly perfect.

"Not at all." Their host turned to his wife. "My dear, you know Lady Villentia?"

"I know *of* her, of course." The duchess's tone was frosty.

Interesting. The addition of the widow to our party must be the husband's idea. Gavin was seized with a crushing thought: *Is Lady Villentia Snodgrove's mistress?* He shook it off. The Duke of Snodgrove was known for his devout leanings.

How is Lady Villentia acquainted with such a man? And is she really here to kill him by his own invitation? Perhaps she has a different target?

Gavin dared not allow himself to hope, but he must entertain the possibility. If danger to the duke were coming from another source, he could not focus solely on the known assassin. Much as her buttons might wink and her eyes hide a well of sorrow.

"I see you have already met your fellow guests. Captain Ruthven, Mr Jackson." This time, the duke's voice was cold.

So, Jack may be the son of a family friend, but his suit is na welcome. And I'm guilty by association, or by birth. There were always some who simply did not like Scotsmen.

Gavin watched closely as the duke gave the widow the tiniest of nods. *Is the duke her employer? Is it possible he knows of his own danger and has hired her as protection? Nay. Such a man wouldna take a lass to bodyguard. There must be somewhat else between them.*

Lady Villentia (a consummate professional) did not acknowledge Snodgrove's nod.

Naught for it, thought Gavin, *I'll have to find out the truth myself. No hardship to throw myself on such a sword – she cuts with a bonnie sting.*

But before he could intercede, Jack offered Lady

Villentia his arm, to the duke's obvious delight.

Interesting.

Gavin followed them all into the house.

Let the game begin.

CHAPTER TWO

A Most Inferior Assignment

The previous night, in a very nice part of London...
Preshea moved unnoticed through the abode of the most popular supernatural in the British Empire.

It shouldn't be so easy to break into the home of a vampire. Especially not this vampire.

Lord Akeldama was known by a select few to be a consummate spymaster, and by everyone else as a renowned fashion icon. The two were intimately connected, of course, but even fewer realized that.

His house, a model of decadence and luxury, echoed with emptiness.

Where are his guards?

There were no stealth bouquets or subversive finials. There wasn't even a yappy dog. Or a yappy drone, for that matter.

Oh, yes! Gibson Moontjoy opens that new opera

tonight. What is it called? The Baker of Little Beasley Preshea gave a delicate shudder. She loathed the opera.

She slid into the vampire's main hallway. The gas was turned down, making sinister shadows out of dancing cherub statuary. Preshea became one with their devilish waltz.

One might think a creature that set no traps had no secrets. But Lord Akeldama held everyone's secrets, even Preshea's.

Foolish old fangs.

She chose the sitting room over the drawing room. This was a private matter, after all. Lord Akeldama kept his drawing room for more showy pursuits.

The sitting room was beautiful – mahogany and brocade furnishings, heavy velvet curtains, and a Persian rug. Everything was trimmed with a surfeit of fringe. She could not make out the colors. The only light came from an old streetlamp through a large bay window. It turned everything brown and yellow.

Preshea settled into the window seat, drawing the curtains closed behind her. She curled up her soft booted feet and pulled off her gloves (both were leather; anything less interfered with dexterity). Lady Villentia had no qualms about paying good money for shoes and gloves – hers must be attractive *and* functional (unlike those of most gentlewomen). She also relished the fact that something had died in order for her to dress properly.

She tucked her clothing under and around. Thank heavens fashion plates were calling for narrower skirts next season. Preshea was petite, and the ridiculously wide silhouette of the last five years did her no favors. Oh, she wore *de mode* and wore it *well*. Such fullness was excellent for hiding things (be they goods or services) but she had never *liked* it, and never wore the cage crinoline. She abhorred the idea of being caged in any way.

Tonight, Preshea's evening gown was of bombazine with braid trim, but not because she was still in mourning (she grieved only when it suited her purposes). No, it was because lady intelligencers required dresses of nonreflective fabrics that did not wrinkle. Preshea's was the highest quality bombazine, with intricate detail around the neck and cuffs. She was no fading flower, even when fading into shadows.

Curled in the corner of the bay window, she would look like a statue from the street, were anyone able to see in. But she was confident that the lamp reflecting off the ripples in the glass, plus the heavy curtains behind her, made her invisible from inside or out.

Two gentlemen alighted from a carriage and walked up the front stairs. The conveyance was expensive and discreet – not Lord Akeldama's (he favored the first but not the second).

One of the men wore equally expensive and discreet evening dress. A gentleman of quality and means but not flash. He wore discretion awkwardly, as ill fitting as a cheap waistcoat.

The other gentleman was Lord Akeldama – an undersized absurdity, all pompadour and no circumstance. He sported a monocle he didn't need, an accent not his own, and an attitude forever tempting disregard. He was also the deadliest creature Preshea knew. And she knew a *great* number of deadly creatures, including herself.

Soon enough, they entered her sitting room. Their conversation was a flow of erudite commentary, moist with the syrup of a superior education.

She recognized Lord Akeldama's melodic tenor with excess cadence. "Please sit, my lord."

Deferential, thought Preshea. *His visitor is a man of property and power or the old vampire wouldn't bother with such niceties.*

"I prefer to stand." This voice was deep and tinged with a quiver of fear or age.

There came the clink of glass decanter on silver tray. "Claret?"

"I think not. How long will this take?"

"Not long."

"Where is she?"

"It's not yet two. *Dear* Lady Villentia is *never* late."

Preshea smiled at Lord Akeldama's confidence. *As a matter of fact, sometimes Lady Villentia is intentionally early.*

"Women are always late."

"Perfection takes time."

"Will she do this for me?" He was nervous about her reputation. Or Lord Akeldama's. Or both.

"If we provide the right incentive, *all things* are possible, even perfection." The vampire liked to play with his food.

"Isn't she required to obey you?"

Behind her curtain, Preshea's lip curled.

"You misconstrue, my dear lord. That *brightest* of jewels is no longer under my indenture. I have *requested* that she attend us, *not* ordered it. She will come because she is bored."

Preshea, annoyed that he knew her so well, nevertheless conceded that this was a fair assessment.

"You could not change the rules?"

"My dearest boy! Seven years and *seven years only* – apprenticing, articling, binding, or indenture. You know that, *you* wrote it into law. *For the protection of werewolf clavigers and vampire drones*, if I remember. It applies to intelligencers as well."

"You have been known to bend the rules to your own ends in the past."

"What a *charming* compliment. However, I would never presume. Lady Villentia values her freedom. She has certainly earned it."

"Flat on her back."

Ah. A man who believes in performance piety.

"Now, now. No call for vulgarity. Isn't that the *exact* skill you wish activated on your behalf?"

She heard a sharp clink. A glass set down hard on a tabletop. The visitor had taken claret after all. "I did not think I would have to woo her."

"Out of practice, are we? Don't you worry, my boy, I am *never* out of practice with wooing. And in this instance, I am moved – *quite* moved – by your plight." Condescension entered the vampire's tone. "You may even find her demands *pleasurable*."

The visitor sputtered.

Preshea decided that she was going to enjoy this.

Whatever Lord Akeldama's friend wanted, he wanted it badly enough to deal with two very tricky devils.

"Of course, there is always the possibility" —the vampire was like a fussy eater, picking at his meal— "she may find *your* troubles unworthy."

"This is an affair of great distress."

"To you."

"My family is—"

"Yes, *yes*. Well regarded, pillars of the community, must avoid all appearance of moral turpitude."

The conversation was becoming dull. *So, perhaps I should provide proof of my skills.* Preshea pulled a sharp silver pin from the end of one sleeve. Good for encouraging werewolves to see her point of view, particularly when applied to delicate areas of the body. She pricked the back of her wrist.

Would it be enough?

"But wait. What blood from yonder mortal drips?" Lord Akeldama misquoted. "Perhaps we were hasty in our assessment of the lady's tardiness."

He drew back the curtain.

Preshea allowed a humorless smile to spread over the tinted perfection of her lips.

"Ah, my *precious* gem." The vampire held out a hand, his fingers white.

Preshea was not afraid of vampires. Or at least, not this one. Monsters came in all shapes and sizes, and very few of them were actually supernatural.

She took his hand and gave him her full weight. He stood her up effortlessly. That was always fun. "Lord Akeldama, I was enjoying your view."

"Not so fine as it might be."

"But sir, the road is very street-like and the conversation scintillating."

He smiled, tight-lipped, showing no fang and no threat. "No need to be flippant, my pearl." He escorted her forward.

His visitor was older, with a linear face. Frown lines marred his wide forehead. More lines were grooved into his sallow cheeks, running along his nose down to the sides of his mouth. He had a full head of grey hair brushed up at the front, and trailing muttonchops. It looked as if a frustrated painter had smeared him downwards.

"May I introduce you to—"

The man held up a hand. "No names, please, until we have an agreement."

Preshea made her voice sweet. "How ungallant. You know practically everything about me. So, I am at a disadvantage."

The man took her small hand, offered naked of its glove. "Lady Villentia, I doubt that is possible."

Preshea looked to Lord Akeldama. "Flattery? I like him already."

She did not like him, although Preshea ordinarily preferred elderly men. They were so set in their ways that they only saw what they wished to see. This meant she could get away with murder. Literally. But this one was frozen solid, and none of his lines were from smiling. His clothes were somber and his neck-cloth tight with Biblical starch. He was lousy with virtuous living and the kind of Christian goodness that delights in self-sacrifice. She would not be able to win easily with him. His rectitude was as much a weapon as her looks, and they both knew it.

No wonder he was loath to employ her.

He dropped her hand a little too soon.

She drew it back to her skirt and wiped it with infinite subtlety and exactly enough motion so that he could not fail to notice.

The lines about his nose deepened.

Thus we understand each other.

"Shall we?" Lord Akeldama gestured to three chairs clustered about an unlit fire.

Preshea walked over and swept her skirts to exactly the correct drape as she sat. She kept her neck long, tilting her head to show her complexion to advantage. No man would ever be allowed to forget her beauty. Especially one she didn't like.

She directed her gaze to the vampire, because this visitor would hate to be ignored. "You're right, of course – I was bored or I shouldn't have come. So, why *have* I come?"

"This gentleman has a conundrum."

"A not uncommon failing among gentlemen."

That drove the man to speak his purpose at last. "My daughter has conceived of an ill match."

"A fortune hunter? How embarrassing, but hardly unique." Preshea made a show of binding her bleeding wrist with a handkerchief.

"I wish you to disabuse her of this notion."

Preshea turned to Lord Akeldama. "Surely, you can find something more worthy of my skills?"

"Unhappy that you won't get to kill anyone, my *ruby*?"

Preshea tightened the knot about her wrist by pulling one end with her hand and the other with her teeth. "Matters of the heart are so dull. Death is *never* dull, except when it is one's own."

The visiting lord looked away, disgusted by her tiny show of violence.

Good, I can't allow him to think me tame. "Why should I bother, my lords? Give me good reason if you want the pot sweet and the lady eager."

The vampire looked her over. "I believe you already have one *excellent* reason – you are intrigued despite yourself."

The lord straightened. "But she just said..."

"I am not intrigued by the daughter's ill choices, but by the father's desperation."

"Ah." The visitor slumped back.

Preshea looked him over. "Saintly Duke Snodgrove. I did not think yours was a family prone to scandal." *Why allow your daughter to entertain a predator? Has she been trapped into an arrangement?*

"You know who I am?"

Preshea tilted her head. "His Grace forgets, information is my trade and I'm a merchant of renown. We may not dance in the same circles, but your sketch has appeared in many papers. *Punch* is not always flattering. But somewhat accurate, as it turns out."

Before he objected, Preshea continued. "I've heard much of your philanthropy. A nobleman who advocates for the deserving poor. You entrance me." She leaned forward, knowing this caused the swell of her breasts to rise above the neckline of her gown. A show of force, Preshea-style.

For the first time, she saw fear in the duke's eyes. "I'm a happily married man."

No man is that happily married.

"And I'm not currently looking for a fifth husband. But one wonders what can be so awful about this fortune hunter that you, my lord, are driven to take congress with a woman like myself. I am, one might say, the very opposite of the deserving poor." She leaned back.

He took a grateful breath.

She followed up her advantage. "Here was I, thinking you magnanimous towards the lower orders. Yet your generosity does not extend to your own daughter's suitor? How hypocritical."

"What do you *want*?" He flushed, a slash of color on those gaunt cheeks.

"Besides a reason?"

"Besides that."

Preshea frowned. What did she want? After four marriages, and four deaths, she had everything in life a woman might desire: titled position, swollen coffers, the freedom to travel, and a world that accepted her because it was afraid of her.

"I suppose it is somewhat satisfying to know that even you, Your Grace, nicest man in London, have a dark underbelly of corruption."

The man in question stood and began to pace. "I protect my family, Lady Villentia. Something with which you've little experience, no doubt. Do you know how many children God has taken from me?

Four. And my dear Constance only recently."

What God has taken, no fortune hunter may covet? "My condolences."

"We did not lose her entirely. She went ghost."

"Felicitations on your family's unbirth, then, Your Grace."

He inclined his head and continued with the living. "Violet is my oldest and perhaps I coddle her overmuch. She's a good gel, fond of gardening. She doesn't know what rottenness may manifest in men and I don't wish her to know. I want him gone in such a way that she will not pine, but instead will feel his leaving for the better. Their parting must not originate with me. I could not stand her resentment."

Preshea had his measure then. *A man who prefers to be the hero to his family and his country.*

Still, she had nothing better to do. "It has been a long time since I meddled in anyone else's romance. This could be diverting, but your reason, Your Grace, is not *my* reason. You still have not told me how I benefit."

"What do you want?" He asked again.

Preshea lowered her eyelashes, enjoying the rush of power. Nothing gave her more pleasure than a man of substance at her mercy. "I'll take it as a debt owed. You're a political force – there may come a time when I need a legislative favor."

Lord Akeldama laughed, a fractured tinkling. "There you have it. The sword of Damocles hanging over your head. She asks very *little*."

Preshea gave a genuine smile. "My *dear* Lord Akeldama, you are well aware that swords were never my preferred weapon." She paused, rearranging her plans for the spring. She had thought to go to Paris to visit a favorite shop that specialized in deadly accessories. That could wait. "So, my lords, where is this evil fortune hunter and how will I be integrated into his society?"

"You should enjoy this, my *sapphire*. His Grace is hosting a *house party*."

Preshea inclined her head. "I do love a house party – all those ill-contained sentiments and simmering resentments. Not to mention a restricted timeframe. It makes for a lovely challenge." She frowned of a sudden. "A ghost, you said? The family maintains remourning for the duration of her resurrection?"

The Duke of Snodgrove looked proud. "Indeed. You have never...?"

Preshea sneered. "None of my husbands did themselves the honor. I've always had to wear deep mourning for the full two years. You are still in weeds?" Custom dictated that the family of a ghost need only wear half-mourning through to the poltergeist stage. Preshea was politely asking after the condition of the household ghost. To throw a house party with a ghost gone to poltergeist would be madness, though entertaining madness.

"She is doing well, all her parts still in place."

"You keep her in state?" Preshea wasn't squeamish. She didn't mind ghosts about, but the recent custom of keeping the companion body on display in the conservatory could get smelly.

The duke wrinkled his nose. "No, we buried her

deep and well sealed in the back garden. She haunts the rear of the house."

"Then you won't take offense if I request my chambers be outside of tether distance?" Preshea did not like unwanted visitors in her boudoir, particularly not the undead.

"My *jewel*, of course you require privacy." Lord Akeldama's tone was knowing.

Preshea did not dignify that with a response. As if she would welcome a man to her bed outside the requirements of matrimony. "Now, I have questions about the other players in your drama."

The Duke of Snodgrove sputtered. "I'm due back at my club."

"You could prepare a leaflet for me on your family and friends, but what I need to know is best not written down."

"Very well." The duke resumed his seat. "The man..."

Preshea held up a hand. "I find it is not the things a gentleman notices that are important to a lady of my accomplishments."

Annoyed, the Duke of Snodgrove allowed her to lead.

Preshea began by asking after the ladies of his household and the female guests. They would be the greater challenge. Men, even men who preferred congress with other men, were easily bewitched. The first because she might make them want her, and the second because she might make them respect her. Women felt little but jealousy and mistrust for Lady Villentia. She could frighten young ladies into obeying her with a few sharp words, but matrons were difficult. *Lord save us all from married women with consequence to protect.*

After discussing the ladies, Preshea ascertained the duke's views on his male guests. Finally, she asked about her target, the fortune hunter, Mr Jackson.

"An attractive, cheerful chap, disposed to be engaging, but lacking in funds, title, or brains."

"Then why do you receive him?"

"He is still a gentleman and a Tory! His father was once a friend, more's the pity. Gambled away his fortune and killed himself with drink. Young Jackson is not so bad, but hasn't two farthings to rub together and is foolish about the little that's left. Not right for my girl."

"I see. Very well. Is there anyone else attending whom you've failed to mention?"

The duke sniffed. "Mr Jackson brings along his friend, Captain Ruthven. A Scotsman, if you can stomach it. I don't know why young Jackson feels the need to foist such a creature upon us, but Violet claims he is amiable and no threat to any of the ladies."

Preshea tilted her head. "He is not inclined?"

His Grace looked startled and then horrified. "Oh, no, not that." He gave a side-eye glance at the vampire (who looked amused) and hurried quickly on. "He is simply not the type who seeks a title and he has no need to marry for pecuniary advancement."

"He's holding?"

"Just so."

"Unusual, a soldier of independent means. But not a rake?"

"Not so I've heard. And I am not so devoted a father that I believe my girls likely to attract a man for any other reason. They're plain, solid creatures, good souls, but not... well... you know."

Preshea followed his meaning. "How came this Ruthven by his fortune?"

The duke grimaced. "Wise on his *investments*. Something in transportation."

"He undertook to *trade* in technology?"

"Yes, what matters this?"

Lord Akeldama remained silent, his bright eyes flashing between them as Preshea conducted her interrogation.

"A made man of modern sensibilities, and you don't see him as a threat? Dearest duke, you *do* need my help. A man like that should make you nervous – such men tend to upset careful arrangements. They know too well their own minds, you see? It's most aggravating."

"You're disposed to believe he'll endanger your endeavors on my daughter's behalf?"

"Not to worry, I can handle Captain Ruthven."

That same night, in not quite as nice a part of London...

The club was louder than usual, the voices smoked by expensive cigars and pickled in cheap brandy. Captain Gavin Ruthven felt no inclination to drink or gamble, so he stood and watched a party of werewolves make fools of themselves over whist.

Werewolves were horrible whist players.

Jack found him holding up the wall.

"So, you're truly coming to this house party with

me tomorrow, old sport?"

"Said I would, did I na?"

"Yes, but I know what you're like. And I really like this gel, Ruthven. Topping filly. As round and comfortable an armful as a..." He floundered. "...perfectly boiled egg."

"You sound like a pining gyte from some yellow novel."

"Well, she is! Not that I've had her in my arms, mind you." Jack pouted. "For she is very fine stock. Duke of Snodgrove's eldest."

"Oh, aye." There was a deal of satisfaction in Gavin's tone.

Jack only smiled wider. "You know I don't have your resources, nor the brains to make much of what little I got."

In truth, Jack hadn't the brains to roast a chestnut without assistance, but Gavin let him blether on.

"I require a wife to take me in hand."

Gavin's mind went a little wild at that statement, although he was tolerably certain Jack was not implying anything. Gavin himself preferred a lady to take him in hand. In the bedroom, mind you, not outside of it.

"Where did you meet this paragon?"

"Yonks ago. Brilliantly, we have a family connection. Our fathers went to Oxford together. Before mine went, you know, totty. So, daddy duke couldn't be too off-putting. But then, worst luck, it was grouse season."

"As it is every year."

"Then partridge season. Then fox-hunting

season. And now it's been a werewolf's age and I'm pining away for lack of her."

"A veritable skeleton."

"Ruthven, you cad! Can't you see I'm perishing? It's been months."

"Remarkable."

"Tragic, rather."

"Nay, lad, remarkable in that you remain constant. In truth, I never knew you could be in love for more than two weeks together."

"Well" —Jack give him a cheeky look— "she is *quite* wealthy."

"Surely, the duke willna condone your suit."

Jack lost his grin. "He's as kind a father as he is a politician, known to permit love matches. One of his sons is recently engaged to an *actress*."

"An actress who began life as an honest gentlewoman. I read about it in the papers."

"Well, he can hardly object to me, can he?"

"He fairly can. You haven't fippence. How will you keep a wife?"

"Exactly why I require one with money!"

Gavin, weak in the face of obtuseness, forbore to mention that perhaps the Duke of Snodgrove's generosity of spirit did not extend to gangrels in pursuit of his daughters.

Jack looked at him with the dead-ferret expression he always got when arrested by some revelation. "Wait a moment there, Ruthven, old pip."

"Aye?"

"Shouldn't you be leaving off the moniker of *captain*, now you've tossed up your colors? Not sporting, what?"

Gavin had no idea where that question came from. He'd resigned months back and seen Jack regularly since. Best not to inquire: Jack's thoughts sprang from a well so deep and dry that to ask after their origin was akin to dropping a pebble in a mine shaft and waiting to hear it strike bottom.

"Fair point, but I prefer Captain Ruthven." *Mr Ruthven was my father.* "It gives me an air of authority."

Jack huffed. "Like you need it, great hulking brute."

"And you, such a wee thing."

Jack guffawed.

They were neither of them small men. In fact, stood together, they were of a height. However, no one ever thought of Jack as particularly tall, while everyone knew Gavin to be a veritable giant.

This was due to Jack's nature – all quick movements and a tendency to slouch that resulted in a boyishly unthreatening aspect. Gavin, on the other hand, took after his ancestors. Ancestors who, his ma joked, when the oxen dropped in harness, would take up the plow and pull it themselves. Where Jack was lanky, Gavin was all muscle. He thought of himself as a gentle giant who must perpetually be reminded of how ill he fitted into the civilized world. A great deal of his stiffness had developed before becoming a soldier. When he first got his height, all knees and elbows, he'd learned that the average drawing room was designed with no other intent than his continued embarrassment.

Jack had a reckless disregard for drawing rooms that Gavin envied and never failed to remark upon. They'd settled into a firm friendship based on mutual abuse, in the manner of most gentlemen.

Jack said, "I shall never frighten small children."

"Oh, aye, whereas they scatter before me."

"You said it, not me."

"Which is why I need the *captain* to help smooth away fear. I dinna have your skill at genial idleness."

"You do like to be productive. A most ungentlemanly quality."

"Ruthven, a word, if you are so inclined?"

Gavin snapped to attention at the voice. "Major Channing?"

Major Channing was too pretty for war, except that his skin was also too clear and his ice blue eyes too bright. Pretty or not, werewolves were made for battle.

"Jack, do you know Major Channing? Major, my friend, Mr Jackson."

The major inclined his blond head, cool but not unfriendly. "Your pardon, Mr Jackson, but if I could steal Ruthven a moment? A delicate matter of state."

Jack nodded, a little put out.

Gavin gave him a raised-eyebrow look of *I've no idea either* and followed his former commander out of the card room and into one of the private libraries.

The immortal shut the door firmly behind them.

"Sir?" Gavin was soldier enough to be suspicious of any summons from Major Channing, especially as the werewolf was currently assigned to the War Office. However, Gavin was also soldier enough to wait for orders.

"Sit down, Captain – this not an official matter."

"Dinna tell me it's pack? Or personal?" If the major did not wish to stand on ceremony, Gavin preferred they get to the point. He settled his big body gingerly onto a spindly chair.

"Neither." The major's voice was shaped by too many teeth and too much aristocratic English blood. Gavin, being Scottish, ought to dislike him on principle. And, on principle, he did. Even for a werewolf, Major Channing's proclivities were questionable, his manners grating, and his personality trying. But he'd died fighting Napoleon, and his soldiers respected him for that, if nothing else. Not many werewolves were forged in battle; most started out as some species of theatrical.

"Weel, then, what do you wish of me?"

"It has come to the War Office's attention that you are to attend a house party thrown by the Duke of Snodgrove."

"The War Office been eavesdropping on my private gab?"

Major Channing wouldn't have had to try too hard, supernatural hearing and all. "It's fortunate that I'm home at the moment to vouch for you. It saves us the bother of having to infiltrate."

"Infiltrate a *house party*?" Gavin could not keep the sarcasm from his voice. "In truth, I did hear invading forces were attacking endless games of backgammon."

"Enough levity." Major Channing had many things, but a sense of humor wasn't one of them.

"Sir."

"We believe the Duke of Snodgrove's life is in danger. We wish you to protect him. And don't go blathering on about how you're nothing more than a retired soldier. I've seen you in action, remember?"

Gavin twisted his mouth. He *had* been about to object. Still, it would alleviate the monotony of the party, if he had purpose. "Verra weel. I'll play at guard duty. But what am I against – amateur or professional?"

"Fenians. So, frankly, anything is possible. They could've hired someone. They could be working for themselves. We know nothing but that they've threatened."

"Why?"

"It's this blasted bill. Why workers want to vote is beyond me. Waste of everyone's time. Snodgrove has come out against."

Gavin, wisely, kept his political opinions to himself. "What else must I know?"

Major Channing settled in to the disclosure with no further waffling.

Meanwhile, back in the nicer part of London...

At long last, Preshea was alone with the vampire.

She did not bandy words. Immortals might have nothing but time to waste on niceties; she was not so fortunate. "What else is occurring here, Lord Akeldama?"

He smiled at her, showing fang. "My *opal*, what makes you think—?"

"Don't play me for a fool, old one. This is hardly worth my time. What do *you* want from this house party?"

Lord Akeldama inclined his head. "I believe there may be an assassination attempt on the duke."

"Why should you concern yourself? He is merely a mortal, past his prime. If he dies, he dies – another will take his place."

The vampire sighed. "It isn't *always* about prey for us, although it may be for you."

The monocle came up, although he seemed to be looking through it at the future rather than at her. "As one of the few progressive Tories with oratory skills and political sway, Snodgrove's death would complicate matters."

Preshea allowed disgust to enter her tone. "You wish me to play nursemaid? Is poison likely?" It was, after all, her forte.

"I imagine something more forthright. He speaks against the Second Reform Act. Its supporters are *enthusiastic*."

"What care vampires for voting rights?"

"You are not a supporter yourself?"

Preshea arched a brow. "For workers' suffrage? Why should I meddle in politics? We women are out of it regardless."

"Curious attitude, *lovely child*." This time, the monocle was pointed at her. "I wish him to remain alive for now. He has a role to play. It's easy to arrange while he is in town." Preshea inclined her head. Lord Akeldama's drones were legion. And nosy. "But the countryside is beyond my control."

"Exactly how I feel about the countryside." She focused on business. "You believe a military approach likely? This visiting captain, perhaps?"

"No, not him." A ready denial.

Is Captain Ruthven another agent or simply beyond suspicion? "What you ask is outside my wheelhouse, protecting a man. What possible remuneration could tempt me?"

The vampire walked to a nearby desk. He moved like silk over satin – by nature, not nurture. A sadness, that, for Preshea would dearly love supernatural elegance, but she was not willing to suffer immortality to get it. *One lifetime is unpleasant enough, thank you.*

He pulled out a stack of papers and showed her the schematic on the top.

She needed no more than a glance.

"You know me too well, my lord." Her voice, despite all her control, hungered. "Is it enough to see him imprisoned?"

"No, but publication would *annihilate* his reputation."

"Sufficient to force him into exile?" Her cheeks tingled.

"Would that be enough for you?"

Preshea considered. "Yes. But I should like to be the one who exposes him. How did you—?"

"You are not, nor ever have been, the only intelligencer in my employ."

Preshea considered her old classmates. *Agatha. Had to be. Oh, how I envy her this victory!*

"Very well. I will keep your politician safe for the duration of this house party. I will see his daughter shaken free of all prospective marital shackles. In exchange, you will give me those documents. And I will use them to destroy my father."

"Lady Villentia, we have an agreement."

CHAPTER THREE

A Scottish Captain Will Not Be Handled

The present, at a questionable house party...

Preshea followed her host into Bickerstung Manor. It was an impressive structure, severely classical in the neo-Palladian style. It suited Snodgrove's stoic persona.

Although he was behind her, Preshea remained painfully aware of the big Scotsman. *Gavin Ruthven. Very Scottish. He sets his brogue forward like a weapon. He doesn't want to use an Eton accent, although I wager he could.*

She had to force herself to focus on the other members of the house party. They were assembled in the drawing room around a cheerful fire – a perfect tableau of aristocracy in idleness. Their clothing was impractical, their conversation superfluous, and their smiles as tight as their collars.

Preshea felt instantly at home. The moment she entered the room, currents of power flowed in her direction. She knew herself to be beautiful, and, in her overly simple green gown, daring. Risk-takers were often respected in a fixed social order, for they courted the edge of propriety.

Always inspire ardor or terror – it matters not which, for in society, they share the same sauce.

Then a certain Scotsman entered behind her and attention shifted. She should resent it, but she understood it all too well. That damnable Captain Ruthven was impressive. It was hard for a Mourning Star to overshadow a mountain. In fact, even now, she wanted to turn towards him as he blithely conquered the room. His technique was amateurish and inadvertent. *How can he not know his effect?*

She forced herself to glance at Mr Jackson, establishing a friendly alliance of strangers in the soup together.

Their hostess commenced introductions. Of course, Preshea already knew the names, but she paid careful attention, charting the flow of expectation and precedence as one title followed another.

Three of the duke's living children were in residence. And the dead one, of course. But as it was still daytime, the ghost was not present.

Lady Violet Bicker-Harrow was plainer than Preshea expected, dark and round like her mother but wearing both in better humor. She rose the moment they entered the room, putting aside a sketchbook upon which, instead of the expected insipid landscape, there was a shockingly scientific diagram of a flower.

She gave Preshea and the visiting gentlemen a curtsey without artifice. Preshea dampened down a strange sadness that her own motives must conflict with this poor girl's love affaire.

"My dear Lady Vi!" Mr Jackson charged across the room to grab her fingers and press them ardently.

Lady Violet blushed and tried, not very hard, to withdraw her hand.

Preshea couldn't help but bless Captain Ruthven for exclaiming, "By fegs, Jack! We've just arrived. Control yourself."

Such rudeness, though warranted, was only to be expected from a Scotsman.

One of the other ladies tittered.

Mr Jackson, shamefaced, returned to the doorway with a hangdog expression. "I apologize, Your Grace – I quite forgot myself, being back in your daughter's glorious presence."

The duke gave Preshea a significant look. She wished he would stop. *He'll botch everything. I know what I'm about.*

"With your permission, young man, my wife will carry on her hostess duties?"

Lady Violet covered her mouth to hide her shock at this blatant rebuke of her beau.

Is that my leverage? Is the very boldness of our Mr Jackson a detriment to his suit? Perhaps I need not intercept but instead encourage him in his foolishness?

The next Snodgrove offspring, Lady Florence, was a livelier version of her older sister. She was practically jolly, with Cupid's bow lips and freckles across her uptilted nose. For all her pleasant demeanor, there was a tension about her shoulders that Preshea knew well. *This one has secrets.*

Lady Florence's bosom companion sat next to her, a Miss Jane Pagril. A pretty brunette with a generous mouth that looked as if it smiled readily.

Preshea suppressed an inclination to dislike both ladies. Cheerful people were abominable.

Lord Lionel Bicker-Harrow, the only Snodgrove son present, was a match to his sisters in the matter of appearance, only a great deal more whiskered. He leaned his stocky frame against the piano where his affianced, Miss Fanny Leeton, palpated melodically.

The former actress stopped her playing to rise and curtsey upon introduction. Her execution was flawlessly subtle. The actress reminded Preshea of her days at finishing school, where she had learned the tricks of the stage from various mistresses of it and received a tongue-lashing every time she did not perform to the highest standards. Believe it or not, Preshea had once not been subtle enough – too quick to show anger, too sentimental in her expressions. Miss Leeton was so easy with her manners that Preshea envied her.

The actress approached. "Lady Villentia, how nice to meet you."

"Miss Leeton, an honor. I've seen you perform. Such skill. Although I am not so fond of the theater as my late husband, and thus unfamiliar with your more recent work." A hit and a hint that Preshea's visits to the West End were not her idea, and that she was not inclined to let an actress forget that she was, in the end, only an *actress*.

Said actress took this barb with grace. "Pity. You missed some of my best work."

"Now, now, Miss Leeton, you are engaged to Lord Lionel, are you not? I should say your best work is ahead of you as wife and mother." Preshea could play the dutiful spouse card as hard as any actual denizen of a happy home.

Hypocritical that the third son should be allowed to marry a theatrical when the first daughter might not even consider a fortune hunter. Of course, the rules dictated that while gentlemen might marry beneath them, ladies never could. Preshea could not be too offended on behalf of the fairer sex. After all, she had climbed the social ladder herself via this exact double standard. Still, the duke's objection to one and favor to the other might be more a matter of address than gender. For Miss Leeton had poise where Mr Jackson had none.

"Well put, Lady Villentia," praised the Duchess of Snodgrove.

"And so sad that you were never blessed." The actress had barbs of her own.

Preshea inclined her head. *Perhaps not professionally trained, but a worthy opponent.* In that one phrase the actress reminded everyone that Preshea was lacking (four marriages, none of them fertile). This cast doubt on Lady Villentia's success as a woman. Of course, she did not know Preshea had taken precautions (children incommoded assassinations).

Preshea pretended injury. "Yes, it is sad."

Captain Ruthven stiffened at the hurt in her voice.

Miss Leeton was as gorgeous in person as on the stage. She was not one of those actresses dependent on face paint. She had a fine straight nose, blue eyes, and a full mouth. Plus – *curse it* – she was tall.

Lord and Lady Blingchester comprised the final members of the party. Lord Blingchester looked like a florid and somewhat surprised codfish. Despite being younger than the duke, he was a devoted companion and political ally. His wife was of that aristocratic breed that specializes in mannish features. Snodgrove had described her as a *good Christian* and Miss Pagril's aunt. Neither of which seemed to her benefit. She was squarish, stoutish, and sported a demanding coiffure.

Lady Blingchester made no attempt to hide the fact that she objected to Preshea's presence, manners, and dress. No doubt she would interrogate her husband that night as to the presence of *that woman*. Preshea was accustomed to being *that woman* in social situations involving the Lady Blingchesters of the world.

Preshea addressed the duchess. "Thank you kindly for inviting me." For the benefit of the others, she explained, "The duke and I are on the boards of several charitable organizations together. I do hope it is no inconvenience, Your Grace?"

Said in front of everyone, there was only one possible answer. "Certainly not, Lady Villentia. You are most welcome."

Captain Ruthven and Mr Jackson made equally

polite murmurs of gratitude.

The duchess moved them on before having to admit that either of the gentlemen was most welcome. "Your luggage is being taken up – shall we go in to tea?"

She led the way to the conservatory. The party trailed obediently after.

The conservatory was impressive, if cold. It was to be low tea, quite relaxed. To Captain Ruthven's evident relief, a number of small sandwiches were laid on in addition to the traditional cakes.

He positioned himself near the food and inhaled more than was polite. He lurked under a palm frond of exactly the right height to drape over his head like a jaunty cap, in the apparent hope that it would hide his indulgence. Preshea found it harder then it ought to be to stop herself from smiling at the big man's antics.

She forced herself to focus on Mr Jackson.

The fortune hunter took a chair near Lady Violet – one of the horrors of a casual tea being that precedence did not hold. The couple instantly engaged in an animated discussion on the merits of bee pollination. Preshea considered joining them, but that would appear ham-handed. She must develop a strategy first.

Instead, she conversed with Miss Pagril and Lady Florence on the upcoming season's fashions. A topic upon which any young lady could opine.

"I like them prodigiously," Miss Pagril said with vigor. "Contrasting colors, excess draping, the gathering of overskirts to the back. It's harmonious."

"I'm in complete agreement," Preshea encouraged.

Lady Florence wasn't convinced. "I do love the swish of a fuller skirt. To narrow them down diminishes a lady's consequence, don't you feel?"

"You support the theory that the space formulated by a skirt provides an aura of moral protection?" Miss Pagril's tone gently mocked her friend's wholesome upbringing.

"Well, yes, I suppose I do."

"I have never subscribed to the cage." Preshea pressed her point through mention of an undergarment, which caused both younger ladies to gasp in titillated horror. "Don't you find a close silhouette more flattering?"

Under the influence of fashion, the youngest Bicker-Harrow was moved to passion. "Perhaps for *you,* Lady Villentia, but we are not all blessed with your fine figure."

Preshea laughed. "I thank you for the compliment, dear child, but I believe you will be similarly flattered by the latest fashions."

"We can but hope," said Lady Florence fervently. "I do not even know if I will be out of mourning by then."

"Will I have the honor of meeting your departed sister?" Preshea felt it only polite to inquire.

"At dinner, most likely." Lady Florence looked saddened.

"At least Formerly Connie does not have to worry about such things as skirt shape." Miss Pagril attempted comfort with levity.

It seemed to work. Lady Florence brightened. "Yes, indeed, she chose a lovely dress for eternity, one of her favorite ball gowns. Perhaps too full-skirted for your taste, Lady Villentia."

"But perfect for her, no doubt." Preshea could make no other remark.

Miss Pagril returned to the coming mode. "I, for one, am glad to know I will not have to continually watch my skirts. I can't begin to tell you, Lady Villentia, how many small tables I have overturned simply by walking into a drawing room."

"Surely you jest." Preshea snapped open a fan, in a pretense of hiding a smile.

"Truly. I am less interested in the current style than in the inconvenience it causes the wearer."

Pity, thought Preshea, *for she could make something of herself if she only tried.*

Lady Blingchester clearly did not share her niece's reticence. Her gown was of the latest design and ill suited to her complexion. *Perhaps Miss Pagril chooses plainer fare in contrast to her aunt? Or perhaps Miss Pagril is of that brash type to declare herself no follower of fashion and, therefore, above it?*

"You do not subscribe to the latest pamphlets from Paris?" Preshea probed gently.

"I find they change more swiftly than I do."

Preshea nodded. "It is better to set trends than to follow them blindly."

"For you, Lady Villentia, but I'm merely an unmarried girl and paid little attention." Miss Pagril was remarkably self-aware.

Preshea tilted her head. "You could aspire to become an original."

This was overheard by the aunt. "Now, now, Lady Villentia, I will not have you encouraging my niece to be fast."

Preshea pressed a hand to her chest. "Heaven forfend! I was merely encouraging her to be fashionable."

Lady Blingchester subsided. "Ah, well, with that I must concur. If only she would take interest, she might make a good match. She is fine-looking, if the gentlemen would only look." She issued Captain Ruthven a pointed glare.

Captain Ruthven had been following the conversation, but bestowing the lion's share of his attention upon dainty sandwiches, not dainty ladies. He seemed startled to be suddenly included.

Preshea seized upon his discomfort. "Yes, indeed, *Captain*. I have often wondered if gentlemen truly care for fashion, aside from the pinks and the drones." The pinks were dandies of the first water, peacocks at play, who paid their dues on Bond Street and showed their wares at Ascot. And the drones followed the dictates of their vampire masters, who insisted everyone be well dressed regardless of gender.

So stalwart a soldier as Captain Ruthven was not to be overset by a direct question. "You see me as I am, Lady Villentia." He waved his free hand up and down his big frame (the other clutched a loaded plate). He was respectably turned out, clean-shaven, but with no particular effort. His cravat knot was a mere gesture. Surely, he could undo it with one hand. And would. *Bad Preshea, do not let your thoughts drift in that direction.* Soldiers, efficient and serviceable in all things, even disrobing. *Now, really, do stop it. I mean it.*

"The fashions of the day are not for me," he concluded.

"Or you are not for them?" She lowered her gaze coquettishly.

He inclined his head. "Just so."

Preshea examined him further through her lashes. His valet cared, for his boots were polished and his trousers expertly cut. Perhaps they were not so tight as those favored by society's elite. Nevertheless, when he shifted, the fabric stretched alarmingly over the massive muscles of his thighs.

Perhaps, Preshea thought, *it is best for my wellbeing that he does not take to a high-end tailor.* If the fabric were to strain any more, she would be hard pressed to keep her gaze away, partly due to appreciation and partly for fear of his seams bursting.

The conversation flowed genially, coaxed along by Preshea and the occasional quip from Captain Ruthven. The young ladies were honored by the attention of a worldly lady, not to mention an *actual* gentleman. Lady Blingchester supervised but heard nothing so egregious it required interjection again.

The Duke of Snodgrove gave Preshea various significant looks, trying to turn her attention to his daughter and her suitor. They remained cloistered together.

The tea was drained with sufficient gusto to be a

balm to the duchess's pride (although the sandwiches were consumed mainly by Captain Ruthven), and the rest of the afternoon seemed set to proceed apace.

Outside, the drizzle became a steady rain. There would be no riding or strolling about the garden. Preshea was pleased, for surely inclement weather would also prohibit assassination attempts of the military variety.

With nothing else to entertain, they agreed to return to the drawing room for an afternoon of cards.

Preshea excused herself on the grounds that she must change out of her travel dress into something more appropriate. In actuality, she needed time alone to collect her thoughts and formulate a plan.

Mr Jackson was not to be taken from his ladylove so soon after reuniting, but Captain Ruthven seemed eager to freshen up as well.

Together they followed the butler. Jennings was respectably stiff but near a hundred in attitude if not actual age. It took him a full ten minutes to hike the stairs. Preshea found herself exchanging amused glances with Captain Ruthven behind the poor man's stooped back.

Their rooms in the guest wing were across the hall from one another.

The butler left, tottering slowly away.

Before shutting her door, Preshea said, testing Mount Olympus, "Enjoy your dainty sandwiches, Captain?"

"'Tis a pain to be a big man in a world made for tottie folk. Miss Pagril frets about her wide skirts, yet I knock things over constantly, skirts or no. My hunger should inspire sympathy, not ridicule."

"And thus I am both chastised and reminded of my own stature."

"Oh, aye, such a wee thing – leastways, you fit into chairs."

Some devil seized her tongue. "Captain, you've no idea! Can you imagine, on more than one occasion, my feet have been known to *dangle*? This very moment, I note that such a large bed graces my delightful room – my only avenue of approach is to run at it and leap in order to gain the top."

He let out a bark of surprised laughter. "I'd offer a boost, but it might be taken as an insult to your good name."

"Or to yours, Captain." *Don't you know? I have no good name.* "To have sunk so low as to be groomsman to a diminutive lady who needs aid not in mounting her steed but her counterpane."

He gave her a sharp look, unsure as to the nature of her teasing. To mention *mounting* and *counterpane* in the same sentence? Preshea was delighted to see him flush about the ears. Perhaps he was not so indifferent to her charms as she thought.

Preshea could not quite countenance her own daring. She was not one for jocularity, but it seemed deceptively easy with him. She was used to gibing at those around her, seeking weakness. So far, Captain Ruthven seemed to have nothing more than a delicate stomach, a supposed clumsiness of which she had seen no evidence, and a delight in dainty sandwiches. To all of which he admitted so readily, they could not be used against him. He was comfortable in his own skin and did not flinch when she ribbed him. It made her quite long to do so.

He gave a little bow, ending their banter. "Weel, lass, I'd be happy to play groomsman if you've need of my services. It wouldna be a hardship." Before she could decide whether this was levity or a genuine offer of a more licentious nature, he left her in possession of the hallway and at a loss for words.

Preshea entered her own room, closing and locking the door behind her. She stood, struck by a sensation of wonder – *I am not opposed to such an offer.* She actually enjoyed imagining him there, bent, big hands cupped, at the edge of her bed. Although, he would need only one hand. She might place her stockinged foot into it, and he would lift her up to the bed with ease. He would be gentle about it. She could tell. That made her shy away. She was not prepared for gentleness.

I am only curious, Preshea told herself, *because I have never before had kindness from a man in my bedchamber. And because gentleness is so alien to my own nature.*

She forced herself to focus, undoing the many buttons down the front of her dress with small, nimble fingers. She should summon one of the upstairs maids, but she needed time alone.

She hung up the green gown. Her trunk had been unpacked, the clothing pressed. The duchess ran a tight ship. Her outfits hung, a cluster of dark dramatic colors. The last husband was three years gone. She was not required to wear mourning, but Preshea liked dark colors. She looked well in them. Plus, they reminded people that she was the Mourning Star.

Abruptly, she shut the wardrobe door and went to perch on her bed. It was high. Her feet did dangle.

For longer than she ought (given the coldness of the room) she sat in her underthings, shoulders hunched down into her stays, arms wrapped about her tiny waist. Mentally, she stripped herself of the longing, bit by bit, as she had stripped herself of her traveling gown.

He would be no different from the others. His tenderness was a front to hide angry force. He was a soldier and he had killed, like her. Once bare of society's trappings, he would be as demanding as any man, as ignorant of her needs, as cruel in his desire. How *dared* she want? To forget the past so easily?

For shame, Preshea Buss. There is no hope to be found in a man. I am done with wanting anything but control.

I will break his heart, she decided. *That is the only way to expose his brutality. Then he will lash out at me as they all do. And I will have my reason for never trying at all.*

It occurred to her to be sad, that she equated her power with his pain. She forced herself to imagine his face if she let him love her and then spurned further advances. She did like him, pathetic creature that she was, and she should suffer for that weakness. She welcomed the bitter pill of self-loathing as an antidote to lust. She would not expose herself again. She would not risk her heart or anything else. Better to be alone.

And yet.

And yet. She could not stop imagining his big

hands under her foot as he lifted her. For he would be gentle. She *had* to believe that. Some man, somewhere, had to be gentle. Why not this one?

I am such a fool.

CHAPTER FOUR

Dangling Feet and Participles

What on earth just happened? Gavin wondered as his valet helped him into a fresh cravat.

Mawkins was a dab hand with the length of cloth and would have taken care with the tying of it, but Gavin grumbled his usual refrain. "I'm a simple man – keep it simple."

Mawkins tutted but did as requested. "Which coat, sir?" He hadn't asked about the waistcoat. Mawkins had stopped asking about waistcoats years before. Gavin was hopeless with waistcoats.

"We'll be at cards all afternoon."

Mawkins selected a refined charcoal frock coat, cut in such a way as to make Gavin's shoulders seem even larger. Gavin thought it a bit much, but Mawkins was never wrong about frock coats.

"Will there be anything else, sir?"

Can you explain to me the workings of one wee assassin's brain beneath the blackest hair I've ever seen? Would it be soft, that hair? I'll wager it's soft. And springy.

"Nay. Thank you, Mawkins. Everything solid belowstairs?"

"Nothing of consequence to report, sir. The odds are against Mr Jackson."

"I ken that's the truth of it."

"Would you like a flutter in favor of his suit?"

"Nay."

"Sir? You know something of consequence?" Mawkins was never one to turn down a wager, especially if he might benefit from inside information. Since he'd started out as Gavin's batman, he enjoyed a level of familiarity with his master unprecedented amongst his peers. Thus, he was wise to the aristocracy.

Gavin explained, "I'm thinking Jack has more than just family set against him."

"Poor Mr Jackson."

"Aye, indeed." Gavin didn't explain further. He didn't know why Lady Villentia was intent on Jack, nor what relationship she had with Snodgrove. He was beginning to doubt she was there to kill the duke. But that might be wishful thinking.

He must conclude that his own feelings regarding Lady Villentia were too confused to relay anything further to Mawkins. The valet was in favor of matrimonial bliss and could prattle on at the slightest whiff of interest. *Sir is such a nice man – why hasn't sir found himself a wife?* Gavin would not be beaten down by his valet. No matter how old a friend.

"Find us a mourning band for dinner tonight, please? There's a household ghost. It wouldna do to be disrespectful."

"Very good, sir." Mawkins collected the travel-soiled garments. "Will there be anything else?"

"You'll manage the claret for later?"

"As always, sir."

Gavin retrieved his current book, in case card games or conversation lulled over the course of the afternoon. He was back downstairs a mere fifteen minutes after having left.

Jack was hovering over his lady, who was busy with her scandalous flower sketching. They were discussing the finer points of herbaceous borders. It was a subject about which Gavin was certain Jack knew nothing. However, ignorance had never stopped Jack from waxing poetical on any subject.

Of course, he searched the room for Lady Villentia, pretending that he was getting a feel for the gathering and watching out for Snodgrove's safety. The resulting spike of disappointment at her absence was ridiculous.

She'd surprised him in the hallway. She'd flirted with him, and not in the calculated manner she threw at others – with those sharp, careful smiles. No, she'd forgotten herself for a moment and given him insight and delight without caution.

He had to wonder. Did her inclinations match his own? Did she wish to be cared for in the way he preferred? His sexual experience was limited to ladies of a professional nature. Yet even the most experienced of his partners had been startled by his requests. As a result, he'd given over finding a lass who might answer his desires in kind. Yet Lady Villentia had appeared almost eager. Should she like it, to be cherished?

He forestalled his thoughts – not right in polite company.

He was disinterested in the game of whist between Miss Leeton, Lord Lionel, Lord Blingchester, and the duke. The two matrons were gossiping softly about who was to be presented at court, a conversation in which he would be unwelcome.

With no other option, he approached Lady Florence and Miss Pagril, who, while disinterested in him as a marriage prospect (thank heaven), seemed pleasant lasses.

They occupied a window seat together and were not averse to his company, if their smiles were any indication.

"Captain Ruthven," said Lady Florence, "are you refreshed from your journey?"

"Aye, Lady Florence. The sandwiches were verra helpful."

Lady Florence hid a smile.

Miss Pagril did not. "Should you like more?"

Miss Florence joined her friend in teasing. "Shall I ring for Jennings? It would be no trouble."

Gavin chuckled, delighted that they were relaxed enough in his company to mock. "I'd as lief na trouble Jennings. He seems the type to mock a lad who canna resist a sandwich."

Both ladies laughed.

They chatted amiably, Lady Florence and Miss Pagril disposed to be charming both to him and to each other.

Lady Villentia took longer than Gavin expected, even for an exquisite. When she finally appeared, she had changed into a dark blue day dress of watered silk. Again it was simple, decorated only with a little fringe about the bodice. His lass seemed to favor simplicity. *None of that, now, she isna mine. I need na pay attention to her preferences, much as I would enjoy it.*

He noticed, attuned after her conversation earlier, that her skirt was narrower than any other present. It flowed out the back, emphasizing her curves. Never one for frills and puffs, he found the dress pleasing. Although he missed those jet buttons.

Lady Villentia circulated, as he had, and drew the same conclusion, joining them at the window. In the hallway, his paltry charm had brightened those sad eyes, but they were dulled once more. He was tongue-tied at the loss.

It fell to the daughter of the house to formulate a greeting. "Lady Villentia, welcome. Is your room to your liking?"

"Very much so, Lady Florence. It is pleasing in both proportion and furnishing."

"Oh, Lady Flo, please. *Lady Florence* makes me feel like someone's maiden aunt."

"Lady Flo, then." Lady Villentia gave a half-smile of genuine pleasure, as if she rarely experienced kindness.

"The bed isna too high?" wondered Gavin,

testing.

"I did not try the bed, Captain." Her eyes narrowed at him in warning.

The younger girls were rendered speechless.

Gavin realized his gaffe. "A wee joke from earlier. Pay me no mind."

Lady Villentia's attention was caught by something outside the window. "Lady Flo, your father wouldn't set his staff to gardening in such a storm, would he?"

"Certainly not."

"Ah. So." She said nothing more, but Gavin strained his eyes to see. Had she noticed someone lurking in the pouring rain? Had she spotted the real assassin or was she deflecting notice? He saw nothing.

"I was pleasantly surprised to find your father kept a dirigible, Lady Flo," commented Lady Villentia.

"Oh yes, Father can be quite avant-garde. Not in his faith, of course, but he does have some progressive leanings. Hides them well, poor thing, but can't seem to stop." She glanced fondly at her father. "We've had members of the local werewolf pack to tea, and I know he meets on business with vampires in town. Of course, such interactions go hand in hand with the latest technology. Do you favor newfangled gadgets, Captain Ruthven?"

The Scotsman gave a rueful smile. "I too was surprised by the dirigible, but na pleasantly. I canna deny it – poor Lady Villentia played witness – I'm a terrible floater."

"He was near as green as Lady Blingchester's

dress." Lady Villentia's tone said much on her opinion of said dress.

The girls tittered, raising their fans to look surreptitiously at the gown in question.

Lady Florence was sympathetic. "I understand your suffering, Captain. Brutal way to travel. And so slow."

"Oh, but it's such fun," Miss Pagril disagreed.

"It's unnatural, taking to the skies," objected Lady Flo. "What do you think, Lady Villentia?"

The widow watched this mild disagreement with interest. She must be noticing the intimacy of the two lasses. The delicate little touches. The way they leaned into one another.

"Are you asking me to render judgment on floating as a practice, or merely my opinion?"

"Both," said Miss Pagril, cheekily.

"Technology is difficult to pause, once it has taken flight. Only ask the Luddites. Floating is here to stay and cares not for my judgment. As to the other, I find dirigibles useful under certain circumstances, when one wishes to make a grand gesture, for example. I knew a gentleman once who floated up to a lady's window, singing an aria, his arms full of roses."

"Oh, how romantic!" breathed Lady Flo.

"What foolishness," objected Miss Pagril.

"Perhaps." Lady Villentia shrugged delicately. "But the lady was impressed and disposed to look upon the gentleman favorably. I call that a good use of a dirigible."

"Was it a beau of yours, Lady Villentia?"

"Of mine? Certainly not. I should never hold with such silliness."

Did she glance in his direction? Gavin was glad. His heart might favor tenderness with the fairer sex, but he was not inclined to sentimental codswallop.

Miss Pagril tapped Lady Flo on the wrist with her fan. "There, you see?"

Gavin was surprised to find he was enjoying himself, despite painful awareness of the pristine perfection next to him. The way Lady Villentia spoke, so careful, so clipped, and yet encouraging. It showed years of training. She smelled of peaches. Was that also training? She was like a white rose, all velvet petals and sharp thorns. But roses did not smell of peaches.

I'm no poet to be hunting lyrical descriptions. I'll learn her given name and then think of her by that. I hope it isna somewhat awful, like Ernestine.

Or Beulah.

Preshea did not expect to enjoy herself. How was such a thing possible in the company of perfectly sweet girls and a perfectly decent gentleman? Well, perhaps not *perfectly* decent. He had wickedness buried within, to tempt her with talk of beds.

As a rule, Preshea loathed nice people. Add to that the fact that both ladies were a full decade her junior, mix in that they were female, and Preshea expected to be anywhere else in the room. Yet there she sat.

She had acquired female friends before, but in the manner by which she acquired pierced ears (necessary for her image and to prove to the world that she could). She never liked them and they had not liked her. They had tolerated her because friendship guaranteed that her cutting remarks were (slightly) more frequently targeted elsewhere.

There was nothing wrong with Lady Flo and Miss Pagril. There was nothing wonderful about them, either. Their manners were neat but their experience narrow and their conversation confined. In short, they were the kind of young ladies whom, under other circumstances, Lady Preshea Villentia would have ignored.

Yet these girls knew who she was and were cordial with no ulterior motive. They showed no inclination to underhandedness. Preshea wobbled on unstable ground. Her instincts screamed to protect herself, to ward off kindness for the cruelty that inevitably followed.

She remained aware of Captain Ruthven, as one might be conscious of the warmth of a fireplace. *Crikey, I'll be toasting bread over him next.* How could one not be aware of the man – he took up so much space.

In consequence, she directed the bulk of her remarks to Lady Flo and Miss Pagril. She experienced unexpected pleasure, watching them blossom under her interest. They valued her opinion. Or they simply didn't want to be poisoned at supper. Lady Villentia's reputation included her preferred methods. The last rumor she had heard mentioned her love of a certain ring. She was wearing it now, under her black gloves, an unassuming onyx-and-silver trinket. It wasn't filled. She never used a poison ring for *actually* poisoning anyone – too obvious. She used it to remind people that she could.

Preshea rubbed the bump of it with her thumb. *When they know more of men, when they are fully out in society, they will not wish to know me. I would hurt their prospects with my sophistication.* Poor little things, they had no means of protecting themselves, no resources at all. She might not have friends, but at least she had training.

I'm going soft in my old age, thought Preshea, and then, *there is definitely someone out in the garden.*

She swiveled to check on the duke. He sat well away from the windows, thank heavens. *Out of shooting range.* Of course, it would take a truly excellent marksman to kill a single person amongst the group sitting in a drawing room, near a window or no. The man in the garden was only watching, waiting for them to leave the house. *If I were a hunter, I should plan around an outdoor activity, one that spreads the party out. Like walking. Or riding. Nevertheless, I shall check that everything is locked down this evening, after the house is abed.*

As to her other assignment: she had put the idea into Lady Flo's head. That a grand romantic gesture, involving something risky, like a dirigible, was the thing to win a girl over. Now she must see that idea spread to Mr Jackson.

Knowing the duke's lack of subtlety, he would

ensure Preshea was seated next to Mr Jackson at supper. She would take that opportunity to begin working on him, encouraging ridiculousness. At the moment, he was waving about a fern frond as if fanning himself. She was inclined to think it wouldn't be difficult.

Preshea was indeed seated next to Mr Jackson, precedence be damned. Over the mock turtle soup, she intimated that a grand gesture was just the thing to set true love aflame.

"Take a stance, you think?"

"Don't you?" It was always best if a gentleman felt an idea were his own.

"She does love flowers."

"My dear boy, she lives in the country, surrounded by gardens."

"Yes, of course. Something more exotic? What about a lobster?"

"A *lobster*?" Preshea, unflappable though she might be, was flapped by this suggestion.

"She was saying earlier today how fond she is of lobster. Perhaps a brace of lobster? Is *brace* the right word?"

Preshea hid a smile in her napkin. "Perhaps not a gift, but more of an action? Lobsters might be considered ambitious."

"Quite right, quite right. Show her I am a man of deeds, not lobsters, what?"

"Exactly so."

"I must ponder further."

"Ponder away, dear boy." Preshea knew her normally cool eyes were bright with merriment; what an absurd fellow.

Mr Jackson's wide mouth relaxed out of its perpetual smile. He squinted in thought. Clearly, devising non-lobster gestures of affection taxed his mental capacities.

A lull descended over the guests as the soup was removed and cod in supreme sauce brought out.

Until that moment, the table had included an empty chair, its place unset. The sun now below the horizon, that chair began to fill with the ghostly form of the deceased daughter, Formerly Constance Bicker-Harrow. The family encouraged their guests to refer to her, rather coarsely, as Formerly Connie.

The ghost, from what one could see of her in the bright candlelight, looked much like her sisters, although thinner and more somber by way of general expression.

How novel – a dour ghost.

Formerly Connie was, naturally, not served. She was included in conversation, however, and seemed fresh enough in her ghostly state to follow most of it. Her voice was breathy and she was wispy about the hair. Preshea was inclined to regard this last as carelessness, or perhaps Connie had been flighty when alive.

The company was impressed by the novelty. Few families could boast a ghost. This daughter must have been quite creative to linger so. It had been thoughtful of the duke to bury her nearby, where she might interact with guests. Although, Preshea wondered if it were not kinder to consign her to a proper graveyard, where she might enjoy the company of other ghosts going through the same experience. After all, no one at the table knew what it was to be dead. In consequence, Formerly Connie had little to add to the conversation.

The company was disposed to be equally impressed by the food. *So it goes. If you are careless enough to die, your merit shall be weighed against the pleasantness of a meal. Could be worse, I suppose.* It was delicious. Preshea was hard put to stick to her regimen. She didn't like to overindulge, but the Snodgrove cook was excellent. There was beef stewed with pickles, stuffed loin of mutton, and roasted teal with sea kale. The afters were equally glorious, comprising apricot venetian creme and almond blancmange, with Stilton for those who preferred savory.

After dinner, it was back to the drawing room for the ladies, where Formerly Connie's tether allowed her to join them. They conversed politely on matters of little interest for the requisite half-hour, at which point the gentlemen reappeared, smelling strongly of cigars.

At this juncture, the party redistributed itself according to taste. With one of the footmen acting as her hands, Formerly Connie played whist with her father, brother, and Miss Leeton.

Preshea spent time with Lady Violet and Mr Jackson, more to appease the Duke of Snodgrove's glares than with any ulterior motive. Nevertheless, she used the aura of conviviality to press him into wild declarations and romantic nonsense, pleased every time he said something that made Lady Violet wince.

"My pearl of the sea," he declared at one point, "I will find for you all the delectables of the briny deep. Have you ever had winkles?"

"Pardon me?" Lady Violet was taken aback.

"Winkles!" said Mr Jackson loudly. "Sea snails, don't ya know? Like whelks, only smaller. Very tasty. You must try them. Next time I visit the seaside, I shall return with a bouquet of the little creatures."

"Oh, dear." Lady Violet was coming over faint. "I don't think. Not a snail. Too far, I'm sure."

"Oh, but my dear Lady Vi, they are dee-lish!" Mr Jackson hardly needed Preshea's encouragement. His boisterousness was doing more to nip the burgeoning romance in the bud than any scheme of hers. Really, even if he were not a fortune hunter, these two were most ill suited.

Lady Violet seemed a sensible little thing. Given time, she would figure this out on her own. Ridiculous of her father not to have more faith in her.

Still, there was the other assignment to think on. Preshea stared out the window a moment, but there was nothing to see; it was quite dark.

She glanced at the window seat, where she had made up the fourth earlier. Captain Ruthven was back charming the young ladies. Miss Pagril glowed under his kind regard. Preshea thought he was wasting his time with that one, although it would be a good match (he had exactly enough money for her lack not to be seen as grasping). For some reason, Preshea found that painful to consider. What had been congenial when she was a participant seemed depressing when she was across the room. *This is what comes of attempting friendship.*

Using the excuse of a long day's travel, she retired just as Miss Leeton sat at the piano. It might have been thought rude, but she didn't care.

CHAPTER FIVE

Ghostly Consequences

Gavin wasn't one to drink every night, in the way of some refined gentlemen, but he did occasionally take a drop of claret in the wee hours to settle his ghosts.

There were some ghosts, like the one at dinner – real, interactive, haunting her old home. And there were some ghosts that haunted a man instead of a place. Ghosts that were made of formless stuff, spirits of a brutal past, undead lurking in corners of men's minds. Especially after war.

Gavin didn't regret his soldiering days. He knew for a fact that he didn't have it as bad as most. Some ex-soldiers drowned themselves in gin. It was cheaper and better at dulling memories than claret. Gavin couldn't abide gin and he didn't require saucing to sleep. His ghosts were only occasional visitors. In the wee hours, they woke him, sweating, with no memory of which battle he'd revisited or whose faces he'd seen damned.

Gavin's ghosts were impressions left on the backs of his eyelids, of werewolves shifting not for joy of the hunt but for war. The sounds troubled him, not the loud bangs but the softer crunching bone that always went with a vanguard of fur, the nighttime attack of the great packs of the Empire. The smell was there too, copper and sulfur, blood and blast. His ghosts were borne aloft on the glory of men's suffering. His eyes popped open to the buzz of fear and anticipation, as if he too might shed skin for the madness of a moon.

Wakefulness was immediately followed by an amorphous feeling of profound loss.

He excused himself that, under such circumstances, a glass of claret was medicinal. Mawkins certainly made no judgments. *For a change.* Perhaps he too indulged for the sake of his ghosts.

Sometimes, Gavin drained the snifter quickly, seeking numbness, and rolled into the less sweat-soaked side of the bed – to dream of lesser ghosts, or better, nothing at all.

Sometimes, he took his claret to the window and stared into the night, enjoying the peace of smaller hours.

And sometimes, he awoke to a restless hunger.

"Dainty sandwiches," he said, into the silent room. *Two bites at most. Cucumber or egg and mayonnaise, the bread spread thick with butter.*

He would not ring for Mawkins. It was gone two in the morning. He would make shift for himself.

Surely, the pantry held something for a man to nibble.

He got himself out of bed. It was a cold night, yet Gavin wasn't one for nightshirts. Mawkins professed to be shocked, but had learned to tolerate this eccentricity. In case of fire or sandwich peregrinations (Mawkins was well aware of his master's habit of midnight food pilfering) the valet set out a banyan.

It was a quality robe, all dark blues and greens, dignified and big enough to cover Gavin entirely, crossing over at the front. Of course, a banyan was considered outdated in these days of smoking jackets and indoor trousers. It had been his father's, but it was such a nice plaid. Gavin thought he looked rather well in it. Plus, it reminded him of his da.

Candle holder in hand, he padded softly downstairs into the bowels of the house, where delicious things resided. He found an apple, a wedge of brown bread, and a bit of Stilton left over from the cheese plate. He ate them standing up like a barbarian, confident that Mawkins would explain the midnight theft so no servant would take the blame for his gluttony.

He was headed back up, passing through the main entranceway towards the grand staircase, when a voice nearly had him jumping out of his skin. And he was a large man; it took a big jump to get away from that much skin.

"Why, Captain, what are you doing out and about at such an hour?" A soft female voice, clipped, pristine.

How could a woman with such white skin be so invisible? He held his candle aloft.

Lady Villentia moved into the light. She still wore her dark blue dress. The watered silk was made for nighttime; it folded into shadow. She had her arms crossed over her chest and was glaring at him, as if it were not more suspicious for her to be awake, about, and still dressed.

"Have you na slept at all?" he found himself asking, worried. Was she ill? Or was she going to kill someone? He considered. It was late. Plenty of time to have killed someone already.

"I sleep very little. Why are you awake?"

"Hungry."

A huff of suppressed laughter. "Of course you are. How silly of me. Hunting more dainty sandwiches?" She seemed obsessed that he liked the little ones. As if she enjoyed seeing him indulge in something incongruous.

"I canna deny I was looking. I like them in triangles, without their crusts. Sadly, none left. I made shift with somewhat less dainty. What are you hunting, lass?" She was hardly after killing the duke, not downstairs.

"Just checking up on a few things."

"Things?"

"You'll think it a girlish fancy, but I like to know all doors and windows are secured before I take to my room. Perhaps I'm of a nervous inclination."

"I verra much doubt that, Lady Villentia. You've enemies so bold, they'd follow you here and invade a duke's house party?"

"My dear captain, did I say they were *my* enemies?"

Gavin felt a sudden surge of joy. Were they on the same side? Had she been charged with protecting the duke as well? He'd never heard her spoken of in a defensive capacity, but society always glorified the bad and forgot the good. Still, he was not so green as to give his own position away. "You're thinking someone is after Jack?"

She blinked at that, uncrossing her arms. The candlelight cast a warm glow over her white perfection. He remembered childhood tales of the sídhe, Fair Folk, and thought for one fanciful moment she was sent to lure him into madness.

"Mr Jackson in danger? Why would I think that?" She did not dissemble or attempt to hide her capabilities with false modesty.

"You've been watching him carefully."

"Poor Captain Ruthven, are you jealous?"

"Verra."

She sighed. "Come with me while I continue my rounds. I'm weary of talking in the hallway like little sneaks."

"Are we na sneaks?"

"Yes, but you, at least, are not little. Snuff out that candle, do." She walked away without bothering to see if he would follow.

He blew out the candle and followed, of course.

She moved without the stiffness that had imbued her whole body in polite company. *A vampire's grace.* But her features had none of the unearthly beauty of that set. She might seem fairy-kind, but she was human. *Nay, she moves like a warrior.* She rolled each step across the ball of her foot, silent, those boots of hers softer than they ought to be. Kidskin, like her gloves. *Who buys kid leather boots?* Expensive taste, for they would split after only a few wearings.

She tested the latch of the drawing room window. The big one. It had never yet been opened for fear of rain, yet she checked it.

"You have no reputation as a bodyguard, Lady Villentia."

"Too true. I am ill suited to the task. I would rather be set to kill than to protect. A great deal easier, don't you find?"

"I wouldna know." He swallowed his shock at her directness.

"No? I thought you saw action, *Captain*. My mistake."

"'Tis na quite the same."

"Killing is killing. Does it matter if it is done in battle or bedroom, so long as it is by your hand?"

"I…" He stuttered.

She paused over the latch of the next window, finding it suddenly fascinating. "Do they wake you in the night – the dead?"

"Sometimes. You?"

"Not so often as I think they should. But then, I knew them all well enough to know they ought to die. You did not have that luxury."

"You pity me a soldier's ignorance?"

"Do you require my pity?"

"Nay. Should you like a boost?"

"What?"

He had shocked her with his offer, so reminiscent of their conversation earlier that day. *Have I really only known her a day?* "To check the transom?"

She looked up. "No. If I needed help up, so would he."

"You believe he is alone?"

"I don't think I could fit through that transom, and in my experience, most assassins are bigger than I."

"Suit yourself." So, it *was* an assassin she warded against. Relief flowed through him. They must be on the same side, protecting the duke. Which meant she was using Jack as a decoy. Or Jack was the reason the duke thought she was there.

Should I say somewhat?

He accompanied her through the library, sitting room, dining room, gallery, music room, conservatory, billiard room, and finally the ballroom. She checked every window and door large enough to admit a man.

"The servants' entrances?"

"Done while you were snacking."

He blushed to think that she'd observed him at his meal. "I didna see you."

"You were not meant to."

"Are *all* the stories about you true, Lady Villentia?"

She frowned. "All the ones that matter, I suppose. Why? Are you curious about anything in particular? Like most ladies, I dearly love to talk about myself."

It was an opening, and she so rarely gave one that Gavin was almost at a loss what to do with it. He shifted closer to her, but not so close as to be a threat. It was more that he wished to know if she were warm flesh or made of ice. "They say you've a poison you spread on your lips. That to kiss you would be deadly."

"What rot – how could I keep from poisoning myself?"

"I would take the risk, even if it were true."

She moved in against him then, fast and unexpected. As though she knew he would not try first.

He was wearing a banyan.

A banyan, for goodness' sake.

Even Preshea's father, notorious for his old-fashioned ideals, had given over such antiquated nightwear.

I will not think of my father now.

Preshea supposed the good captain had not realized it, but the darn thing was slipping. Had been slipping all along – slowly opening down the front as they padded about the house together. *And why did I invite him to join me? Because I want him to see me as deadly? Because I want him to know and be proud of all my abilities, not simply the tricks I show polite society? Or because I want to see if a glimpse of truth will frighten him away?*

The banyan was open enough to show all his neck and throat, thick and strong. It exposed his jugular, so vulnerable, and his collarbone, so fragile, even on a man of his size. She could see a sprinkling of chest hair.

"Are you wearing anything under that quaint old robe of yours?" she questioned idly, crowding into his warmth.

"Nay, lass, but I'm thinking…" He trailed off, for she had touched his neck – a feathering of fingertips at the suprasternal notch. His Adam's apple, just above, bobbed as he swallowed.

"You're not cold?" Her voice stayed calm.

His caught a little. "Nay."

Preshea liked that she could make him nervous. He stood there, so big, and yet entirely at her mercy. More than he realized, for there was a tiny blade up her right sleeve. She could snap it out easily, with a flick of the wrist. She didn't, but it felt good knowing he was defenseless under her touch – innocent.

"*Leannan sìth*, I'm at your mercy," he breathed.

How had he known? She almost jerked away, but now it had become a test of her mettle. She increased the pressure of her fingers. "What does it mean, *leannan sìth*?"

"Fair Folk. Pale from living underground – beautiful, lethal. Occasionally, they send forth a lass so bonnie, she inspires mortal men to greatness or despair. I'm thinking you're one of them."

"Are they powerful?" Preshea stroked a single nail along his neck, as if it were the path of a blade.

"Verra. They drive most men mad."

Preshea felt a funny pang at that statement, but she kept the banter light. She moved her hand then and tried to bracket his neck with it, as if to strangle him. She couldn't, of course; her hand was too small (with neither the strength nor the span). In fact, it was a less deadly place for her hand to rest, as she could no longer flick out her knife. But to him it would feel more threatening.

She knew because she felt him swallow again, under her palm.

"I shall try to keep you sane, Captain Ruthven."

"Will you be kissing me now?" he wondered.

"Should you like it if I did?"

"Verra much."

She stood on her tiptoes and braced one hand on his shoulder, the other on his wide chest.

He bent down. He had to; even on her toes she wasn't tall enough. He waited, though, for her to begin. How did he know how much she needed that patience? How important it was for him not to be just another man who wanted to consume her?

She kissed him. Softly, mouth closed. He kept his closed, too, lips relaxed. He held himself still, as if she were a skittish wild creature who might dash back underground to her fairy kingdom. *Ridiculous man.*

She pulled back.

He did not grab. He did not mash his mouth to hers in an excess of passion.

It was glorious.

"Weel, then." He breathed out the words. His eyes gleamed as he examined her face. She could see it even in the dark, but it was not avarice. It was bubbles of joy, as in a glass of champagne. He was pleased. He liked what she had done.

Preshea felt oddly proud. An academic achievement, like the first time she had mixed the perfect dose of arsenic. She wanted to give him something as a reward for his restraint, for surprising her.

"It's my first kiss, you see? Don't look so disbelieving. I know what you think – four husbands. I should say instead that it is my first kiss freely given. Thank you for not demanding more."

He tilted his head.

She noticed then that his hands were on her back. Not fierce or rough, simply there, keeping her balanced. Comforting.

"I shall kiss you again now. To ensure I have the way of it." Preshea suited her actions to words, reckless with surprise at herself.

He let her, of course.

But the *of course* was not because he wanted her, although there was little doubt of that. She felt it against her stomach as she rested flush against him. No, the *of course* was because she was beginning to get the impression he would let her do most anything she liked to him. Not because he was frightened of her, but because it was his nature.

This character flaw was a window of opportunity she should exploit... professionally. But instead, she found herself moving restlessly against him, kissing him deeply – with no ulterior purpose but to find out if his lips really were that soft.

They were and they parted slightly under hers, an invitation, should she choose to take it. Nothing more – no press of slavering tongue, no pull of hands. He did not even rub his hardness against her, although he must be desperate to do so. All her husbands had.

She pulled back and, in the spirit of being daring,

asked him to explain. "You are not unaffected. Do you hold yourself in check because you think I will fly away like a startled bird? Or are you lazy about this kind of thing and prefer the lady does all the work?"

She felt his rumble of amusement, for her one hand was pressed against his naked chest. Surprised, she realized she had entwined her fingers in the soft hair there.

He let the laugh puff out. "Neither. I hold back for love of waiting. Na so I might charge in later – dinna mistake my meaning. When you are ready to tell me what you wish, I will give it to you. Simple as that. Dinna fret – I work hard if you put me to the task, Lady Villentia."

Preshea's grin was only slightly carnal. She loved his answer. A realization that turned her cold with fear. She dropped her hands and broke the moment. Horribly confused. What a terrifying – and tempting – man.

"Don't be silly, Captain. I believe at this juncture you may call me by my Christian name."

"I dinna know it, lass."

"Nor I yours."

"Gavin. Tis na all that much, but it was my father's and it suits me well enough."

She allowed a tiny smile. "It does that. I am Preshea."

He grinned, a bright joyful thing. "Preshea. Perfect."

It was perfect. She was perfect.

How had she known that it had to be she who kissed him?

Why bother with how she knew – she knew and she'd done it. And it was perfect. *And I was her first.* He smiled at that glimmer of susceptibility.

He wondered where they would go next. Would she invite him to her room? No, too soon, if ever. She was afraid, although not of him, not really. She was frightened of something he represented. Not one to admit to that, she might become cruel in recompense.

A challenge, but a bonnie one. Fortunately, Gavin was equal to a courtship where he could not demand with all the self-righteousness endemic to his sex. He preferred coaxing over insisting. He was optimistic – she evidently wanted him. Her breath had hitched and she had caressed him without realizing it. And she had kissed him a second time. He'd thought he would only warrant one before she fled. But there had been another, as if she were testing his resilience and her control over him. Glorious.

And, better still, she had not yet fled. *Strong stuff in this wee warrior.*

"I do not think this is the done thing, for you two to be here in such a way." The voice was unexpected, querulous and breathy with no breath at all.

They had forgotten that there was one member of the Bicker-Harrow family guaranteed to be awake at this hour, with nothing better to do than drift about, looking for trouble.

"Formerly Connie." Preshea pulled away.

I can call her Preshea now, in my head at least.

Gavin said, "I do apologize. You are correct. Such behavior is uncalled for."

Formerly Connie was drifting, her thin arms crossed. "I'm no proper chaperone and this is neither the time nor the place for such carrying on."

On the contrary, thought Gavin, *'tis both.*

The ghost continued her lecture. "I've heard of assignations, but I hardly require a demonstration." She acted as if she were a governess and not a virginal chit half their age and dead.

Gavin saw Preshea take offense. He interrupted before she might say something not rash but overly cutting. He doubted Preshea was ever *rash*, but they needed the ghost on their side. "Lady Villentia is my affianced. We've na made the matter public. You must na blame her. I persuaded her to come down here. I couldna bear to be parted from her a moment longer."

The ghost was mollified. "Well, if that's the truth of it."

"It was naught more than the most chaste of kisses."

The ghost bobbed as if in thought. "I did note that. I must admit to some wistfulness. I never got a first kiss myself."

Preshea smiled. "Were it possible, I should recommend the captain. He is an excellent starter."

The ghost, rather than taking offense at such a shocking offer, gave a tinkling laugh. "Young lovers. Too sweet. Yet in company, you pretend not to know one another."

Preshea made good work of that opening. "It's

my father. He disapproves the match. We must keep it hidden until we can run away to Gretna Green."

"Oh, how romantic." The ghost clasped cloudy hands together. She was still very much a *nice* young lady, with all the Gothic notions of unrequited love to go alongside.

Gavin turned pleading eyes on Formerly Connie. "You will keep our secret, dear lass?"

The ghost straightened, as much as a wispy bit of aether given form could straighten. "I shall."

"We will not embarrass you again by invading your solitude with our trysts." Preshea took Gavin by the hand and led him firmly away.

Out of tether distance.

He followed.

Of course he followed. He would follow her anywhere she wished. He was horribly afraid, after very little acquaintance and two tentative kisses, that he was falling in love with her, which meant following was his only choice.

CHAPTER SIX

Riding Lessons

During the trip upstairs and back to her room, Preshea put more than simply physical distance between herself and the captain. He had carefully not overwhelmed her, yet she felt as though she were drowning. He hadn't pushed, yet she was at the edge of a precipice. The horrible thing was that she knew she could pull away. He would let her.

Preshea leaned against her closed door and listened until she heard his shut. She felt as if she might cry. There was something so perfect about him. But *perfect* for a Preshea four husbands ago, when she might have learned to love and value such a man. Instead, now she would always be waiting, expecting him to turn into them.

She knew this was a weakness in her nature. She was rejecting something outright that might well be the saving of her. Not saving her soul, or her heart, or anything so trite. But *her*, the decent human part of her, the tiny pieces that were left. Yet she hadn't the courage to overcome what other men had done to her. They were dead and gone, leaving no ghosts to haunt her. She'd given each his two years in widow's weeds, black to mauve, for a death without unbirth. And they'd left her alone and drained, picked over, rotted to the bone exactly like them. She honored their memory by making an altar out of her inability to trust.

Preshea spent the next few days avoiding Captain Ruthven, applying the skills of her trade in order to do so. She'd been in subterfuge as well as murder. Even at a house party of confined society, it was easy to be unavailable or perpetually conversing with others. No doubt Gavin was startled by how well one female with the right set of skills could avoid contact with a man who had no artifice at all.

The second week started out much the same as the first, alternating between whist and loo, absent of late-night kisses. Breakfast was casual, luncheon was civil, and supper was formal. The storm outside increased in ferocity, turning into a veritable gale.

Preshea took every opportunity to coax Jack into ridiculousness. She also managed a private discussion with Lady Violet. During this exchange, she insinuated much about the poor quality of Jack's offering, not as a suitor but as a man. His buffoonish ways were to be pitied. Surely, *dear* Lady Vi wasn't *serious* about the unfortunate creature? As the older woman, Preshea felt it her duty to speak with censure on the subject of young men who waved dried flowers about willy-nilly and pressed a girl's hand. Fervently. In public!

And so forth.

This met with modest success. Lady Violet was the type to be impressed by the opinion of others, especially when such an opinion was expressed in a sympathetic manner.

Preshea, having found the house's security up to her standards that first evening, did not feel the need to make such a thorough check every night. But she did walk the windows after dark, to see if she might catch anyone looking in. She took pains to avoid encountering other members of the house party, living or dead. Now that she was on her guard against Formerly Connie's wispy ways, it wasn't difficult. She saw Miss Leeton once, paying a late-night call on her affianced (actresses!), and Mr Jackson heading down to the kitchen upon some seafood-related quest. She did not encounter Captain Ruthven alone again.

Gavin.

She wasn't certain whether she was grateful or disappointed. Nor did she know if he searched for her, padding about in his ridiculous banyan, hoping she might catch him.

She thought about it. But resisted.

Gavin was wounded by Preshea's coldness. He thought of her as two people now – the Lady Villentia she played to an audience, and the Preshea she had allowed him to glimpse late at night. Preshea had sad eyes. Lady Villentia had a maddeningly clipped voice. Preshea had kissed him in the dark, frightened by her own daring, sweetly hesitant. Lady Villentia ignored him in the grey day, perfect nose tilted up.

Both of them watched the duke and the windows.

Of course, he'd gone looking for her the following night. And the night after that. And the night after that. He'd hoped to find Preshea going about Lady Villentia's business, willing to crack her icy surface just for him.

He caught glimpses of Preshea occasionally – a hint across the room while she chatted. Those eyes, always wary, would alight briefly on him and shift. But not in welcome. He was no longer permitted in her circle. Oh, he could walk over, join the conversation. But then she would mysteriously not be part of it, her attention straying towards the piano or a game of backgammon. She was not cutting him. It was not so overt that anyone else noticed. Only that wherever he was, she was not.

It hurt. Naturally it did, because with two measly kisses, he was more intrigued by this widow than he'd been by any lady of his acquaintance, ever. But he knew why she was doing it. He'd seen such before, and he cursed the husbands, for one or all must have been brutes. How dared they dull such sharp perfection with misuse? Somehow, he must prove that she'd nothing to fear from him.

He watched her watch their host. He watched their host watch Jack. He watched Jack watch Lady Violet. And he watched Lady Violet, more often than not, watch the floor in embarrassment. Jack's antics were becoming extreme with desperation. Lady Violet's interest waned accordingly. Poor Jack had never learned that what could be charming during a ball became gauche over long rainy days in the countryside. Perhaps Preshea encouraged Jack in his foolishness, but it took so little effort, she was wasting her talents. Poor Jack was quite equal to ruining his chances without assistance.

The morning of the ninth day of Gavin's punishment (as he'd come to think of it) dawned cheerful and sunny. This was a joy to all, for they'd begun to believe they'd be confined indoors for all three weeks.

The ladies of the party, after breakfast, resolved to take a walk. The gentlemen, even lovesick Jack, declined, ostensibly because they felt their boots might get smudged. In reality, Lord Blingchester required a respite from feminine chatter.

Gavin couldn't blame him. Lady Blingchester would try the patience of a saint. Her strident voice more often than not complaining – about the weather, the food, or her own perceived ill health (although to Gavin's eyes, she was rudely robust). She directed the bulk of this putrid flow at her husband, who looked as if he'd started life a jolly chap, but had deflated after marriage.

As a general rule, Gavin was disposed to be kind to the fairer sex, but Lady Blingchester had made her dislike of Preshea evident. Gavin, while realizing his lass did not give two figs for such a woman's good opinion, was not unaffected. He liked watching Preshea charm everyone, yet Lady Blingchester would not be charmed.

So it was that the ladies – the Duchess of Snodgrove, Lady Blingchester, Lady Violet, Miss Leeton, Lady Flo, and Miss Pagril – sallied forth into the sunlight, parasols raised against it, enjoying the delights of a world washed clean.

Preshea stayed behind. Because the duke stayed behind, and Gavin was convinced she too was charged with his protection.

Lord Blingchester grumbled at the cursed addition of a female to his much-desired peace and suggested a game of high-stakes cards. Preshea was clearly not frightened by vast sums recklessly changing hands, but she also did not attempt to participate. It being a game for four, Gavin left the others to it. Poor Jack was abysmal at cards, and what little funds he possessed were bound to be lost in the space of the two hours it would take the ladies to walk the grounds.

Gavin opted to relax near the fire and read the *Mooring Standard*, all the way from London, only two days old. He wasn't really reading it, however.

Preshea stood looking out the window. There wasn't much to see; the gardens were ill tended, with nothing in bloom. Yet somewhat had caught her attention. That perfect face was arrested in an expression of … wistful pain? It was irresistible.

So, he went to stand next to her and look as well.

She tensed and then seemed to give an internal sigh and let him stay, sharing her silence.

The ladies drifted about the grounds outside. The duchess, Lady Blingchester, and the older girls had attained a goodly distance and were striding towards the fields beyond the gardens. Miss Pagril and Lady Flo, on the other hand, had decided against such a robust endeavor and deviated to amble through the maze, arm in arm. There was nothing so spectacular about this undertaking that it required Preshea's focus.

"You dinna wish to join them?"

Preshea did not turn. "I am content here, thank you."

It rankled. He wanted her to notice him. "You're na the type of lass with many female friends?" It was not a question, but he raised his voice at the end as if it were, so it came off less insulting.

"I attended finishing school. Long ago. There were girls there as those two are."

He narrowed his eyes, wondering at her implication. He'd noted the affection between the two youngest ladies. They acted as lovers might, but he didn't know how worldly Preshea was in that regard. Especially since he'd felt how tentative her kisses were.

Fortunately for him, she continued. "Girls who had such friendships that they could finish each other's sentences. How terrifying it must be to trust anyone that much. And yet I happen to know that even now, twenty years on, they are still friends."

She looked at him, finally.

He kept his face calm and open. "I've sisters. They're considerable loyal to their pals. I'm na one of those lads who holds that only men may enjoy true friendship."

Preshea returned her gaze to the window. "I have always preferred isolation. Less chance of betrayal. Occasionally, as I get older, I wonder if perhaps it might once have been worth the risk."

"You're na so old. There is still time." He wanted to wrap both arms around her and pull her close to stop the sadness she did not show.

"I think not."

"You might let them in a little, tell them somewhat more about your life. Those two – Miss Pagril and Lady Flo – they wouldna judge harshly." Really, he was saying, *You could tell me more, you could let me in, I wouldna judge.*

"You think there is something to judge?" She twisted his meaning.

"I think that you believe so." He twisted it back.

She shrugged. Her fine white shoulders rose and fell against the lushness of her gown. It was blue again – a deep, rich velvet, cut tight everywhere it should be tight. It was trimmed about the neck, wrists, and ankles with white muslin so fine, a man might think those parts were see-through. He suspected she wore it during the day because it would be too visible at night with those touches of white. What a remarkable woman, that he should judge her fashion choices thus, without flinching.

Gavin left her to her wistfulness and returned to his newspaper. She needed to feel his lack much as he'd felt hers over the last week.

Jack, having lost all his funds and not so dim as to dip into imaginary coffers, came to join Gavin.

"Anything interesting?" Jack was chipper for a destitute.

"Lost your shirt, laddie?" Gavin tried a diversion, to avoid admitting that he'd not been reading the paper.

"Lost your heart, old man?" Jack shot back quietly, tilting his head to where Preshea was now perched in the window seat.

Perceptive blighter. Jack was a buffoon, but he wasn't stupid.

"She is bonnie." Gavin refused to be bullied into a confession.

"You and I, old pip, have encountered many beautiful women in our day. You've never watched any of them when the *Mooring Standard* was to hand."

Gavin passed over the paper with an amiable curse. "You take it, then."

"Serious, is it?" Jack took the newspaper. "Stronger men than you have tried and failed with that one. Or tried, succeeded, and died. I know you court danger, soldier and all, but don't you think that's a bit much? Man wants something in his arms, I understand that. And she is quite *something*. But could you sleep at night? Put your slipper wrong and you might not wake up."

"It'd take a more serious offense than slippers."

Jack snapped open the paper, indicating that he'd said his piece.

Gavin took the point. Were he interested, truly interested, in becoming husband number five, it would be well to know exactly how (and why) the other four had died, first.

The weather held, and the company being restless, it was decided they should go riding that afternoon. Preshea did not like the scheme, as it would put the duke in danger, but she'd no ready excuse to keep him indoors.

Lady Blingchester, a renowned horsewoman, had brought her own mount. Her husband developed a headache and decided to nap, but she and Miss Pagril were eager to ride.

"No Lady Flo?" Gavin inquired politely as they walked to the stables.

Now that Preshea knew his name, she'd a difficult time not using it. It suited him and she liked it. It was softer than Ruthven, which sounded as it if might belong to a sinister vampire in one of Radcliffe's Gothic tales.

Miss Pagril shook her head. "We are not attached at the hip, Captain. Although it may sometimes seem thus. She doesn't ride. Whereas I, particularly at my uncle's estate, find riding a great comfort."

Gavin nodded sympathetically. Preshea suppressed an odd affection for the nape of his neck, exposed with his head bent listening to the girl.

I'm going mad.

Preshea did not keep a horse and was no great

rider, but she'd learned the basics. She asked the
groomsman if he might bring her something staid
from Snodgrove's stable. A docile bay gelding was
led out. He was enormous but (the man assured her)
sweet as a lamb.

Mr Jackson proved to be even more useless on
horseback than she, but not so inclined to admit it.
Rather spitefully, Preshea thought, the duke ordered
up one of his son's mounts. His middle son, mind you,
the one in the cavalry. The horse was a high-spirited
chestnut stallion with a fine sleek neck and fire in his
eyes. Mr Jackson seemed more struck by the fineness
than the fire.

"Jack, my lad, you dinna want somewhat
calmer?"

"I can handle him, Ruthven! He is a first-rate bit
of flesh, isn't he?"

"Aye." Gavin did not roll his eyes. Preshea
thought that quite noble of him.

The captain's mount was a huge, rangy gelding,
ugly as sin and common as muck. But Preshea was
not so ignorant she couldn't see that the beast had the
bone structure of a god and the affectionate temper of
a lapdog. That horse would trot for days, never
stumble, and put on speed without whip simply for the
joy of it. Gavin must win many wagers against foolish
gentlemen who could not see past the shaggy exterior
to the smooth gait and perked ears of a goer. She
lowered her eyes to hide the glow of approval. How
like Gavin to choose a horse for temperament and
ability rather than appearance. The stable lads patted
the beast with real pleasure. She noticed Gavin tipped

them generously for their affection as well as their care.

Preshea allowed two groomsmen to assist her into the saddle. She'd no pride over skills she'd taken no pains to perfect. Frankly, those skills she'd perfected must be kept secret, so she rarely got to glory in them. Yet there was Mr Jackson, lousy with self-satisfaction, trying to master a horse beyond his capacities.

Said horse reared. Mr Jackson's normally cheerful face was grim with determination.

Lady Violet, mounted on a pretty dun mare, observed her lover's antics with ill-disguised horror. "Oh, Mr Jackson, really! Formerly Connie's mare could use the exercise – why don't you ride her?"

"Listen to the lass, Jack." Gavin swung himself up with ease.

Mr Jackson ignored them both.

How foolish men are! To insist on being experts when they have no truth to draw upon, and risk their necks besides. Perhaps that is why Gavin is drawn to me – I'm like his horse, only ugly on the inside.

To lighten the mood, and because she was kind, Miss Pagril took pains to draw Lady Violet's and Gavin's attention away from the spectacle of Mr Jackson. The unfortunate chap was now making an ass of himself trying to mount unaided. The chestnut kept sidling.

Miss Pagril said, "Captain, why do you call Mr Jackson by his Christian name? Isn't that unseemly?"

Gavin obliged her by drawing his horse alongside. "You're thinking he's Mr Jack Jackson?

What cruel parents would name a bairn so? Nay, his given name is Clydeward, if you would believe. *Jack* is a wee version of his family name. He much prefers it."

Miss Pagril did not try to hide her smile. "I can see why."

Finally, Mr Jackson was mounted and they headed out. The Duke of Snodgrove and Lady Blingchester led. Lord Lionel, Miss Pagril, and Captain Ruthven followed with Lady Violet, and Mr Jackson at the rear.

Preshea encouraged her horse to join the elders at the front. She did not want the duke too far away. He glared. She was supposed to be supervising his daughter. Preshea met his eyes and gave a tiny shake of her head. He subsided, but remained displeased.

They rode through the grounds and farmland until they reached a little wood.

"Might we go around to more open fields?" Preshea requested. "Surely, the woods will be full of fallen branches. I'm afraid I'm no horsewoman to jump and maintain my seat."

The duke dismissed this. "Pish-tosh. Anything in the path will be small enough to walk over. I wish to see the state of the lumber after such a storm."

Preshea sighed. She'd tried.

She moved up until she was as close as possible to the duke, muscling Lady Blingchester's spirited mount out of the way with her bigger bay. The bay hung his head in shame.

Lady Blingchester snorted. "Some people are nothing but social climbers. Come, Jane, Lady Violet,

let's ride the outskirts. I could use some speed. Your Grace, we shall meet you on the off side."

"Watch those fields," warned the duke. He was examining an old oak that had lost a branch. "Gets marshy after a rain. I wouldn't push past a canter."

Lady Blingchester wheeled her mount and took off. She really was a bruising rider. Lady Violet followed. She didn't have quite the seat of Lady Blingchester, but she stuck it well enough to impress Preshea.

"Jack, I wouldn't," warned Gavin.

But Mr Jackson also maneuvered about, yanking hard on the reins and kicking with both legs as if riding a recalcitrant donkey. The chestnut galloped off. By some miracle, Mr Jackson stayed in the saddle.

Gavin looked as though he wanted to go after, but then he glanced at Preshea and noting her close proximity to the duke, stayed.

Now a diminished party of five, they wended their way into the trees.

Preshea knew exactly the most dangerous point. She would have chosen it herself, were she a gunman. To one side of the path a mound of boulders rose up, with bushes at the top, forming the perfect cover and vantage point for a man to lie with rifle braced. No doubt the other side was sloped, easy to run down. The path widened just there, making the riders entirely visible from the outcropping.

Preshea saw a glint of light off the barrel and launched herself at the duke just before the shot rang out.

CHAPTER SEVEN

The Efficaciousness of Muff Pistols

Preshea had kept to the duke's right so that her sidesaddle pointed her whole body in his direction. Consequently, all she need do was push forward off her mount, grab onto as much of Snodgrove as she could, and drag him to the forest floor.

Which is what she did.

He bellowed at her in annoyance.

The shot reverberated through the air.

Preshea was pleased. She and Snodgrove were safe between their two horses while bullets whizzed overhead.

Until the duke's horse bolted.

Her own mount, sweet-tempered and placid, rolled his eyes to the whites and shifted from hoof to hoof, but otherwise stayed still.

Preshea cast herself over the duke, shielding him

with her body. Well, or some of him; he was a deal taller than she.

She heard Miss Pagril give a cry and shifted to see the girl's horse bucking before taking off pell-mell. Miss Pagril stuck like dried porridge even as the beast leaped fallen trees in a wild gallop.

Lord Lionel gave a cry and took off after her, no doubt intent on effecting a rescue.

Gavin was off his mount, hand tight up the reins at the shaggy head. His horse must have seen action, for the gunshot had barely rattled him.

"Preshea!" Gavin cried.

"We're fine. That rocky hill, there. A rifleman. Go!"

Sensible man, he took her word as truth and, dropping the reins, ran up the promontory. Or perhaps it was simply that a soldier found it easiest to obey orders? That impressive physique of his wasn't for show, either. Once he got moving, he was fast!

"Are you injured, sir?" Preshea asked the duke, evaluating him for blood and finding none visible.

He attempted to sit up.

"No. Stay down for now." She pressed a firm hand to his back.

"What are you about, woman?" He wasn't hurt to be so grumpy. "What on earth is that?"

Preshea had out her pistol. Hadn't even realized she'd drawn it. She kept it hidden away in a special pocket in one of her petticoats. It was a tad indelicate to get at and occasionally bruised her leg if she wasn't paying attention when twirling, but she preferred not to go without.

No pretty pistol with gilt metalwork and mother-of-pearl handle for Preshea. She favored a six-shot revolver, no frills, no decoration. It was viciously practical, hard steel with a plain rosewood grip. Preshea was no expert markswoman and no gun fancier to care for looks. She wanted something light enough to carry and small enough to hide, which shot a bullet in the direction she aimed, and was easy to clean afterwards. She didn't use it much; hers was not a directly confrontational lifestyle.

She held it now, comforted by its presence and pleased to see respect in the duke's eyes.

"You do realize, Your Grace, that not everyone likes you?"

"Are you one of those people?"

"Don't be absurd. Even if I were, hired gunmen are not my cup of tea."

"Well said."

There was a shout from Gavin and another shot, followed by some crashing, and then a howl of rage.

Preshea glared at the duke. "Get off the path, and for God's sake, *stay down.*" She stood, shielding herself with her horse, then pulled the reins over the docile creature's head and dropped them down to the duke.

She didn't wait to see if he followed her instructions. Keeping her gun steady, Preshea marched up the hill after Gavin. It was muddy and her velvet riding habit was never going to be the same, but sometimes sacrifices must be made.

Weel, she's definitely na the assassin. Gavin's heart expanded in relief.

He fancied he acquitted himself well from Preshea's vantage point, although he was more winded than he liked. *I'm getting old.* He dashed over the hill to find, as she'd said, the rifleman.

He was sprinting down the other side to where a little dirigible was moored, bobbing softly. Gavin yelled and cursed.

The man turned, hoisted his rifle, and fired in one smooth movement that spoke of professional training. *I could've used a man of such skill in the Crimea.*

Gavin registered only that much before heat scalded his upper arm. He gave an animal roar (more of frustrated surprise than pain).

Curse it. He's getting away.

The man swung himself over the lip of the gondola. Floating wasn't the fastest method of escape – a horse would be quicker – but it was effective. Plus, Gavin realized, once the enemy cast off and started to rise, he could turn around, rest the gun on the lip of the basket, and fire once more.

Which is exactly what the bastard did.

Gavin rolled.

Dirt spit up where his head had just been.

Bloody good shot. Gavin wished with a passion that he'd his own rifle. *I'm also a bloody good shot.*

Two pretty kid boots appeared in the corner of his vision.

"Temper, temper." Preshea did not look down at him.

"Good afternoon, Lady Villentia. Know this

laddie, do you?"

She was holding a ruthless-looking little revolver. It was small enough for a lady but big enough to pack a punch. "Not my kind of training. More your people's."

She raised both hands, took careful aim, and shot.

Her bullet embedded itself in the gondola of the dirigible.

The aircraft bobbed higher.

Gavin sat up and held out a hand. "May I?"

With an expression that might have been relief, Preshea passed it over. She dusted off her hands on the rich brown velvet of her skirts.

The gun was lighter than Gavin expected. "Rimfire?"

"Of course."

"American?"

"Naturally."

"That's not verra patriotic." He needed only one hand to aim such a featherweight. Good thing, too, for the other was currently useless. He was also feeling slightly light-headed. Surely he wasn't losing that much blood?

Gavin shot, getting close enough to the rifleman to splinter the gondola's railing in his face. Deciding on caution over killing, the blackguard hunkered down, his gun with him.

"That one is soldier-trained," said Gavin.

"The War Office needs to get its house in order."

Gavin wrinkled his nose. "Can't keep record of them all."

"No? Pity."

The airship floated higher, caught a stiff breeze, and began drifting away.

"We should set someone to track him from the ground." Preshea took her gun back from Gavin and set it down within easy reach of both of them. Without asking, she bent to his upper arm.

He craned his neck to see. "Bad?"

She cut away the cloth of his shirt and coat with a wicked little knife. "I'm sure you've had worse."

He had. This one was a shallow dig through the flesh of his upper bicep, not bad at all. It was bleeding, of course, but not so much as it might have elsewhere.

Preshea picked up her revolver and wiggled the hot barrel at him. "Cauterize?"

"You canna be serious, woman! It's na the bloody Dark Ages!"

"No need to be crass, my dear captain—"

"Gavin," he grumbled at her.

"I'm only trained in limited field dressings, those designed to keep a girl moving."

"Curious training, for a lass."

"I disagree." She lifted her skirts at that and began fishing about under them. She showed no embarrassment and a good deal of shapely leg. She was wearing bloomers, of course, but only to the knee, and she'd fine white stockings below. *If I stroke with one finger, might she excuse a wounded man?*

His thoughts were arrested by a ripping noise. "What *are* you doing?"

"Tearing a strip off my chemise. Needs to be clean for field dressing. Cauterization may be out of date, but I assume that truth still holds?"

Practical lass. The hem of her petticoat was muddied from the terrain, so she needed to reach farther up to get at something unsoiled.

Triumphant, Preshea produced a length of fine muslin, beautifully embroidered. The chemise she'd just casually destroyed cost more than his favorite boots.

"Would rather enjoy you in your best underpinnings than have you rip them apart for a mere scratch."

"Don't be ridiculous." She began wrapping his arm, efficiently but with unexpected solicitude.

"It is a *mere scratch*!"

"I know that. What's ridiculous is the idea that I should be wearing my best underpinnings when riding!"

"Nay?"

"Certainly not."

"You've finer than this?" He fingered the end of the bandage where it now dangled. She'd done an excellent job with the dressing, although she'd tied the tails into a bow.

She narrowed her eyes at him. "What do you take me for, an amateur?"

She was so close.

"Of course na – silly me."

His arm now smelled of peaches, her scent on his bandage. "I canna ken how you smell so delicious."

"Delicious? What are you, a werewolf?"

"Preshea?"

She looked up from his injury at last.

Blue, her eyes are blue. The deepest, darkest blue

Gavin had ever seen.

"I'm thinking that a kiss would make it better." Gavin felt his request was greatly daring – her gun was still within reach. He'd wager she didn't miss at close range.

"Thinking that, are ye?" She imitated his brogue and didn't reach for her gun.

"Fair certain."

"Well, if it'll help." She suited her actions to her words with a quick, sure kiss.

He let her try to make it brief, but then opened to her, waiting to see if she would take the bait. *Vulnerability, retreat – is she hunter enough to chase? Aye, she is that.* There came her tongue, only the tip, tentative. Then he felt a little sigh against his lips – the puff of acceptance.

Their kiss paused naturally, at the place where it could have gone further. He might have relaxed back against the earth, which he now realized was cold and damp. He might have caressed one stocking-covered leg. He might have coaxed her to lie atop him, kiss him more deeply.

Her eyes said she might have agreed.

But they heard shouting and the sound of horses galloping in their direction.

Preshea reached for her revolver, licking one finger to spit-test the heat of the barrel. Finding it cool enough, she flipped down one of her petticoats (Gavin was mighty disappointed) and stashed the gun away somewhere uncouth. Brushing down the rest of her riding habit, she stood and offered him a dainty hand.

He took it but didn't use it to rise. He didn't need

it and likely would have overbalanced her with his weight, the laws of physics being what they were. He took her hand so he might stroke the back with one thumb. So he might feel how strong it was.

To his surprise, she smiled, gave his fingers a squeeze, and then let him go.

"We should return to the duke. I have a feeling he might require an explanation."

Everyone who could had come to rescue them. Those cantering the fields heard the gunshots and raced back, except Jack. Lady Blingchester reported, snidely, that the foolish lad had fallen shortly after the party split, and returned to the house.

Miss Pagril and Lord Lionel also did not return. One assumed she had allowed her horse its head and they were already home. Gavin didn't fret, for she was a fine rider.

The duke's mount was gone and he was grumpy about it.

"He'll return to the stables," Preshea consoled him. "I shouldn't worry. If not, we'll send out a search party of groomsmen. Meanwhile, you take my mount and I'll ride double with Captain Ruthven."

"Are you mad?" objected Lady Blingchester. "That's most unseemly!"

Preshea said, without inflection, "In case you hadn't noticed, we are short a horse and the captain is injured. Someone must keep him in the saddle. What if he becomes dizzy from blood loss? Since I applied

the dressing, it should be me. Unless the duke wishes
to do the honors? Lady Violet is *certainly* not an
appropriate choice. Are you offering, Lady
Blingchester? I should struggle with your horse – too
much mettle for me – but if you insist. Although I'm
the least likely to be an additional burden to the
captain's animal."

Gavin was impressed. She'd complimented Lady
Blingchester on her riding and insulted her weight in
the same breath.

Of course, his wonderful Rusticate, being a
gentleman steed, would not protest any added burden
– even as much as Lady Blingchester might entail.
And Gavin had not lost that much blood. But he dared
not open his mouth to protest her scheme. After all, it
would net him Preshea in his arms for the entire ride
back.

He was in luck. With no further objections, the
duke assisted Preshea to mount before Gavin. She
perched there, stiff. He held Rusticate back to take the
rear of the party.

Once the others were far enough ahead, she
allowed herself to relax against him. He pretended it
was out of affection, although it was likely so they
could talk quietly and not be overheard.

"I intended no insult, Captain. I know you could
stick your horse, but this seemed the easiest solution.
I'd like the duke back at the house quickly."

"So, you *are* here to protect him."

"You too, I take it?"

He nodded. "Fenians."

"Reform League is what I was told." She leaned

her head back against his collarbone, on his uninjured side. He rested his cheek against the crown of her head.

"What's daft is that Snodgrove is na the worst to stand against them. In February, he spoke for leniency. He's a moderate."

"Can one really be progressive and a Tory?"

"The duke's a special breed of bagpipe."

He could feel the movement when she shrugged.

"Perhaps it's a violent faction of the League? He was seen lunching with Adullamites."

"Careless lad."

"Very. And he is too good a speaker. My sources tell me it is his rhetoric they fear, not the man himself. We should send someone after the attacker."

"Aye. I'll put Mawkins on it."

"Your batman valet?"

"Aye."

"But won't you get awfully scruffy without him?"

She was teasing; how fine a thing. He was not above teasing back. "You ken I need a shave of an evening?"

"I *ken* no such thing! I meant *scruffy* in terms of wrinkled coattails and ill-tied cravats."

"I can shift for myself if left clear enough instructions." Gavin brushed his chin against her glossy hair. It was braided and looped for riding, soft against his skin. "You lost your hat."

"That happens when one launches oneself off a horse at a duke."

"We shouldna have left without looking for it."

"It is of no consequence." She tilted her head even farther back and brushed the tiniest of kisses on his chin. "Stop mussing my hair."

"'Tis remarkable. I didna think tresses could be so black outside the West Indies."

"Are you likening my hair to that of a heathen?" She pretended offense.

"And your eyes are blue." He couldn't stop his tone from sounding petulant.

"Well, yes, yes, they are."

"'Tis disconcerting."

"Sorry if the color offends – not a great deal I can do about it. Yours are blue, too, you do realize?"

"We'd make beautiful blue-eyed bairns."

"What a thing to say!" She twisted in token protest, but not so much as to jostle his injured arm, which he'd rested about her waist. *'Tis the most comfortable position.*

Rusticate twitched an ear at their antics but kept plodding along. The horse was keeping the others in sight but had allowed distance to develop, as if aware of his master's desire for privacy.

Preshea changed the subject. "Remarkable beastie, this gelding of yours. Doesn't look like much, but he's a work of art underneath, isn't he?"

"Aye." Gavin's affection for the woman in his arms expanded. The way to Gavin's heart had always been through praise of his mount. *Weel, and dainty sandwiches.*

She quieted a moment and then said, very softly, as if to herself, "Quite the opposite of me."

"Now, lass, I'm thinking that's somewhat for me

to find out on my own."

"If you must."

Preshea had to accept that they were on the same side, which made the big Scotsman an ally of a kind. *I can no longer avoid him. How very vexing.* Why hadn't Lord Akeldama said he'd double-booked? Unless Gavin represented a different interest. The werewolves, perhaps? *Immortals, always mucking about in mortal business.*

To Preshea's annoyance, the rest of the afternoon was spent fussing.

The Duchess of Snodgrove fussed over her husband. Lady Flo and Miss Pagril fussed over Captain Ruthven. Preshea retreated to her chambers for a nap, claiming fatigue over the excitement of the afternoon.

She watched a man who must be Mawkins (he was riding Rusticate) depart the grounds. He galloped back a good while later, empty-handed. The duke's attacker had escaped.

Preshea did not return downstairs until well after the dressing bell chimed.

She was never alone with the duke long enough for him to interrogate her, which was perfectly fine with Preshea. It was most likely that, having tried and found Snodgrove well protected, the enemy would not try again during this house party. Certainly, the duke would not take another silly risk.

Preshea sighed as the maid helped her into a grey

dinner gown. *The rest of my stay is going to be awfully dull. Unless, of course, I do something to liven it up.*

Gavin had made an offer. *The question is, do I take him up on it?* Preshea had never engaged in a dalliance before. At least, not one of this particular nature, with no ulterior motive. *I would be pursuing nothing but my own pleasure. I would be using him. That's appropriate for a woman like myself.* She tried to console herself by reasoning away her desire.

Would the experience be good for me or ruin me in some way? If I found I liked it, or liked him, more than I thought myself capable, will it destroy my future plans?

Oh, really, Preshea! she reprimanded herself. *What plans are those?* She'd served out her indenture to Lord Akeldama. She'd done her work for vampire and by royal decree. *I've killed for them both and been well compensated for my trouble.*

In truth, she'd given little thought to her future. *I could retire to the country. And do what? Take up bee-keeping?* She shuddered. *Perfect my badminton game?* She shuddered again.

Is that all that motivates me now? Boredom?

The idea was appealing. It implied that she was attracted to Gavin not for him but for lack of something in herself.

Except that it *was* him. The size of him. The easy way he rode. The comfortable nature of their discourse. He'd never questioned her actions, not once, during that fight. He'd been a partner. It had been easy. *Too easy.* And he was easy to trust, and lean against, and caress. *Too easy there, also.*

There was Miss Pagril to consider. Was she trying to catch him? She was a pretty girl, vivacious, exactly innocent enough to tempt a man to marriage. She would make him the perfect wife.

Preshea was never one to let another lady win, no matter what the prize.

Boredom. Attraction. Curiosity. Competition. Do I really need a reason to take to his bed? What am I actually afraid of?

That he will change me. That he will make me regret my choices. That I will hurt him simply by acting as I have always acted. That in letting him love me, I become responsible for his emotions.

For some reason, the large, amiable Scotsman was the first man Preshea had ever met whom she did not wish to break.

Terrifying thought indeed.

Preshea left her room to make the rounds early that night. The house was silent and still, everyone abed. All the windows were shut. She encountered Formerly Connie in the drawing room, the fire cooling in the grate.

The ghost nodded to her. "Can't sleep?"

"Yes. Then I remembered that my scarf was down here." Preshea had taken to leaving accessories behind of an evening, with this excuse in mind.

"Try a glass of hot milk," suggested the ghost, floating serenely.

"Do you find yourself calmer now than when you were alive?"

"Naturally. Not a great deal to worry about, you understand? Already dead."

"I do understand. Thank you for the advice. Good night, Formerly Connie."

"Good night, Lady Villentia." The ghost drifted away.

Not so bad for a dead thing, as dead things go.

Preshea paused on the stairs when she heard the whisper of cloth. Someone else was awake and about. Someone else *living*, to be precise.

Preshea melted into the shadows.

Miss Pagril was creeping along the hallway, a candle held low, the light shielded with her free hand. Fortunately, she was not heading downstairs; instead, she hurried into the south-facing wing where the family slept.

She moved badly, like one mocking stealth. Although Preshea supposed that was how laymen did it.

Miss Pagril paused at a door and then let herself inside. Whoever it was must be expecting her, for the door was unlocked.

Preshea frowned. *Whose room? Ah. Lady Flo's. Very interesting.* She shook her head in wonder. *Young girls these days are getting very bold.* It put the iron into her. *If Miss Pagril can do it, so shall I!*

Preshea glided down the north-facing hallway and then stopped as Miss Pagril had, in front of a room not her own. It also wasn't locked.

Gavin was awake and waiting for her.

CHAPTER EIGHT

A Scotsman Without His Banyan

"I was hoping you might come." There was a hint of surprise in his voice.

Good, I shouldn't want to be predictable. Preshea locked the door behind her. To keep others out or to prevent herself from fleeing, she wasn't certain which.

She hesitated, watching him. He was sitting on the edge of a bed as big as hers. He'd one of the lamps lit for reading. It cast a gentle light over the room. His fire was built up, cutting through the night's chill. It was all quite welcoming. *Comfortable.* Which made her uncomfortable.

He gave a tentative smile. His chin was shadowed by a day's growth of beard. He was wearing that banyan again, looking like a laird from olden days in some Highland castle portrait. It had slipped again, too, showing his chest almost to the bottom of his sternum. It stopped at the exact spot where she'd been taught to wedge a knife. There had been a deal less muscle on the mechanical construct she'd learned on. Really, what right had any man, even a Scotsman, to that much muscle? His chest hair glinted golden in the lamplight. The quilted fabric of the banyan, thin with age, draped intimately against his thighs. The sash about the robe held it closed, but not so well when he was sitting; it parted over his knees. He clearly wore nothing underneath. *Barbarian.*

She did not move, frozen with her back to the door. This was not something for which she'd been trained. Not exactly.

"You've done this before, aye?" He patted the bed next to him.

Preshea remained motionless but for her mouth. "Four husbands, remember?"

He stood and came to her. His legs were no longer visible, but that chest... The chest was advancing. She forgot to breathe a moment, riveted.

Slowly, softly, he took her small hands into his large ones. "Yet you're shaking, lass."

His thumbs caressed the backs of her wrists in small circles. She was still wearing her gloves, but the skin underneath tingled from his touch. It was an odd sensation – both comforting and exciting. She breathed in shallow sips of air, for he smelled too good, all warm spices like a ginger honey cake.

Preshea considered how she would answer him. With this man, perhaps honesty might work? "I never wanted it with any of them."

"Oh, lassie." There was a world of understanding and, oddly, pain in his response. "In truth, we men take too much, too often. It need not be so." He rotated her hands, palms up, so he could begin unbuttoning her gloves. Before he did, he caressed the undersides of her wrists with one finger. He looked into her eyes then, asking permission. She swallowed and nodded. Then watched the tiny buttons in his big fingers, mesmerized. He was so very delicate and careful about it.

"Perhaps someday you'll keep them on for me? But na tonight. No barriers between us tonight, eh, lass?"

"Already, you believe you will get a repeat performance? You must have great faith in your persuasive abilities."

"Aye. I'm a gruesome optimist." He tugged off the first glove and began working on the second.

"All men, I think, are takers." She pulled her hands away, liking it too much, and removed the second glove herself.

He loomed over her, as comfortable in his skin as he had made the room. He did not press or crowd her in any way. She wanted to pet his chest, following the opening made by his robe. She wanted to press her lips into his hand, to test the meat of his palm with her teeth. She wanted – so badly, she actually ached with it.

Instead, she moved away to sit at his dressing-table, busying herself with taking down her elaborate hairstyle from dinner. *So many pins.*

"Some of us would rather be taken, lass. I hope

so, at anyroad. I canna be the only one. Here, let me."
He knelt behind her. He was so tall that when she sat
on the low stool, he was of a height to still reach her
hair.

He combed through it with those big fingers,
finding the pins and pulling them out. Occasionally,
he would pause and massage the base of her neck with
his thumbs. It was glorious. She watched him in the
looking-glass. It scared her, how big her eyes were
and how much she enjoyed the service – so much
different from when a maid tended to her coiffure. She
had never before met a man who would consider
doing such a thing. Yet he seemed to enjoy it, the little
frown creasing his broad forehead from
concentration, not distaste.

Preshea let her head tilt forward and closed her
eyes, not wanting to stare and not wanting to
calculate. Simply wanting to enjoy.

He finished and the cool weight of her hair fell
against her back. He ran his hands once more through
the strands, swirling against her skull. It was a
glorious relief from the pressure of coils and twists.
Slowly, he pushed the mass aside and over one
shoulder. She felt a kiss, feather-soft against her
exposed neck.

"What do you like, Preshea?"

"What?" The question floored her.

He laughed – a little huff of breath against her
skin. "In this, I ken you may be more experienced than
I. Four husbands, remember? I dinna have any wives."

"But you have had lovers?"

"Only two. I'm hoping they taught me well."

It was an odd thing for him to say. As though a man were to learn anything of his own pleasure from a woman. The very idea! Men were born knowing, and demanding. Were they not?

She turned to him on a breath. "I don't know. No one has ever asked me that before."

He tilted her chin up and looked into her eyes. It was not uncomfortable, but she felt scorched through from the heat there. "Come, then, lass." He stood in one smooth movement, towering over her. "Shall we find out?"

Preshea blinked at him and his proffered hand. If this was what he wanted, she would play along, attempt to fathom his reasoning. Did he desire her loyalty? Why else care for her feelings on the matter of bed-sport? She was there, willing enough; he could do as he wished. Unless she decided to practice her more deadly arts, of course.

She placed her hand in his and allowed him to pull her to her feet. His grip was solid, more rough than a gentleman's ought to be, but sure and kind.

"You are very beautiful." His blue eyes gleamed. She had not thought blue could be a hot color, until now.

"I know."

"But, I'm thinking, damaged?"

Preshea smiled. "Better to say *deadly*."

"Aye, that too."

"You are a brave man, to take me on."

He chuckled. "Or a bun-headed one. Maybe I've an overblown opinion of my own abilities."

Preshea cocked her head. *Is that was this was*

about? Is he a prideful lover? That she could cultivate. "Shouldn't I be the judge of that?"

"Nay, little trickster. You'll na manage me so easily."

That startled her. It was the first time he'd acknowledged that he saw her wiles at work. It was unbalancing.

"Very well." She allowed a little of her frustration to show. He still held her hand but had not drawn her against him. She wanted his warmth. "What do you desire of me?"

He smiled and for once, she thought he might be quite handsome. He certainly wasn't beautiful. In Preshea's family, they were all beautiful, even her father. Gavin's face was too harsh. But when he smiled, the white of his teeth and the crinkles at the corners of his eyes softened it to comely.

Still he held her apart from him, as if waiting for a cue.

"What do I do?" Preshea asked, for once in her life at a loss.

"Be still, simply stand there a moment. I want to look at you."

She swallowed, nervous.

He kissed the backs of her hands, sweet and courtly, although perhaps there was a flick of tongue. She gasped and then laughed at her own surprise. He smiled and paced about her, arranging her hair to fall back. He stroked her arms, exposed by the shorter sleeves of her dinner dress and the absence of gloves. He entwined his fingers with hers at the last, a brief squeeze of reassurance. She felt goose bumps, although she was not cold. She reached to unbutton the back of her bodice, contorting her arms, needing to do something to take back control of the situation.

"Can I help with that, lass? Ask me and I should love it more than anything."

She cocked her head on a sudden understanding. *Of course. It's all my choice. That's his point. And, for some reason, he needs it.* She dropped her arms to her sides. She took a breath, slow, steadying. Her eyes had gone dry from staring as he moved about her. She blinked to moisten them and took another, deeper breath. *Control is something I am good at.*

"Take my dress off me, Gavin."

He unbuttoned the bodice down the back, tiny caresses as he went, peeling it away and laying it reverently aside. Then he untied her overskirt, pulling it up over her head. He was careful about her hair, smoothing it after, his hands wide and worshipful. He lifted up her top skirt, paying it equal attention. Were his hands shaking slightly? Preshea found relief in knowing he was not unaffected. He was pulling off her first petticoat now, and Preshea was beginning to regret that fashion called for so many layers. His reverence now felt achingly slow. He unwrapped to savor, like a poor child with only one gift at Christmas. She willed herself to enjoy, allowing the spice of him to season her confidence. He moved on to her second petticoat, this one heavy with her revolver in its special pocket.

He smiled at the weight.

"Such a canny lass you are, *leannan sìth.*"

He was standing before her now, his eyes warm

as they flicked over her face and neck, her bare arms, and her fine silk underpinnings. His skin was warm too, as his hands stroked the path of his gaze – the side of her throat, the turn of her shoulder, memorizing her with his fingertips. Even that damnable spicy scent of his was warm, inviting. He was one massive, muscled invitation.

He made quick work of her corset cover so that finally she stood before him in nothing but chemise and stays, stockings, drawers, and boots.

Well, I suppose that's still quite a bit of clothing.

"Wait." She stopped him before he could continue.

He froze gratifyingly quickly, a slight panic in his eyes. As if he were afraid she would flee.

"You first," she said instead, accepting his invitation.

He flashed one of those big sincere smiles and, without hesitation, shrugged out of his robe. He was, indeed, quite bare underneath it.

"Oh, my." Preshea's prior experience in such matters had all been beneath nightclothes, at best uncomfortable, and at worst agonizing. She had neither seen nor wanted to see any of her husbands naked.

Gavin was different. Whatever he'd done with the Coldsteam Guards had clearly involved a deal of physical labor. The hair on his chest shaped down to a single line over his stomach. She would not allow her eyes to follow it farther, not just yet.

If I'm going to take advantage of this man, by George, I shall do it properly. I'm no lily-livered milk-

water miss!

She stroked his chest with one hand. Not quite daring enough to go lower. Although she did want to know what he felt like everywhere. *Soon.* No doubt he would allow it. *Soft.* His chest hair was very soft. He closed his eyes to savor her touch. Preshea allowed herself to look at everything he offered. He was not a particularly small man anywhere, as it turned out.

She glanced up to find him watching her. Eyes still so warm, crinkled at the corners in delight at her appraisal. At her obvious interest. At her desire. So, she looked her fill again, flushed but sure. If he was hers for the taking, he should know that.

He was not embarrassed to be naked while she remained clothed. If anything, he seemed to enjoy it, if his cock was anything to judge by.

She found herself smiling. *An odd sensation right now.* Strange that humor should accompany such an act. But she couldn't help it; she was delighted with him. And with herself. And with her power over him. She stepped away slightly and turned around, presenting her back to him and drawing her hair forward over her shoulder. "My laces."

He loosened them quickly. Showing a depth of experience with corsetry that belied only two paramours. Or perhaps each had been for a long duration. He was clearly a man who enjoyed the titillation of undressing his lover.

He guided her around to face him once again so he could pop open the busk. Pulling the corset off and laying it aside, he loosely encircled her in his arms. Instead of pulling her into a full embrace, he rubbed her back, strong and firm, stroking the places where the lacing had bit through her chemise to mark her skin with wrinkles.

It felt so glorious, she moaned and relaxed forward. Her focus shifted to those big hands massaging through the thin silk, although she was acutely aware of his eager flesh pressing against her stomach. She let herself melt, pressing against him. Warm.

Tentatively, she nuzzled her nose into his chest hair, soft and only a little pricking against her face. His breath was rougher now, and his heart, under her cheek, was racing. That plus his stroking hands were causing her own breath to hitch, her body to ache in ways both pleasant and anxious. She was bathed in the scent of him now, and she did not care that it could overwhelm her. She knew she could stop this at any time, the moment she felt close to drowning. And he would let her. But for now, she would be *warm*.

After a long moment, he judged his ministrations complete and let his hands drift up her back, into her hair, to cradle her head against his chest.

She grinned. She had his measure now. "My chemise," she ordered.

He lifted the garment easily over her head. He was so much taller than she that he barely had to stretch. This one *was* her best chemise and she saw him finger the fine silk admiringly.

Now she was standing before him in stockings and drawers, feeling exposed but also even more powerful, for his breath was uneven and his eyes dilated.

"You are so verra bonnie." His voice was roughened by need.

She opened her mouth to say something flippant, but...

"Aye, you know it weel. But you dinna know it from me."

He began petting her naked skin with those big hands. The length of her arm. The base of her throat. He stroked down to her breasts. They were not very big but, she thought, they were well shaped. He seemed to agree, weighing and cupping them in an appreciative way, not critical. It was odd; they felt heavier at his touch, swollen. Her nipples peaked and burned. He pinched them both, very slightly. A sensation, a little like electricity, sparked through her and down to her groin, and she gasped. Her knees actually became weak. It was ridiculous; she was stronger than this.

"You like that."

Preshea only stared at him, eyes wide.

"You may ask me anything you like, lass. And, in truth, ask anything *of* me."

"May I do it to you?"

"Aye, I should like that."

So she did, pinching his nipples, gasping in surprise when they tightened under her fingertips.

"I enjoy it. As I enjoy the little noises you make. See?"

He gestured down. If anything, he had gotten harder. Preshea swallowed, uncomfortable. She wasn't certain she liked the reminder. That particular part of a man's anatomy had never brought her much pleasure. But then, neither had a man's hands. He distracted her by pinching her nipples again, a little harder this time.

There came that tingling flash in response.

I must want him. Strange sensation – a thrill of anticipation combined with moisture between her legs. She had never felt it before.

Unexpectedly, he dropped to his knees before her. It was perfect.

He unlaced her boots, one at a time, then slid them off. Hands squeezed away the ache of confinement. She braced herself easily on his broad shoulders, and he looked up at her, eyes filled with joy at her casual use of him.

Boots placed carefully aside, he rested his head against her stomach, above the ties to her drawers. He seemed to want to breathe her in. He closed his eyes, rubbing the roughness of his cheek against her belly. Preshea ran her fingers through his thick hair.

"Gavin?" She didn't know what she was asking, but she must break the tension; it was too much.

"Aye?" His voice was a low rumble.

"What do *you* want?"

"Ask me that tomorrow." He pulled back a little to untie her drawers; fingers poised and eyes questioning, he waited.

"You may."

He pulled the laces and smoothed the silk down her legs to pool on the floor. His hands slid back up, caressing her legs with the same long strokes he had used on her back. His thumbs leisurely circled her hipbones. She jerked, sensitive there.

"Someday," he said, "you will stand like this and I will lick you here until you come apart above me." He touched her very softly at her apex with one finger.

It was an utterly startling offer. Preshea was humiliated to find herself become wet enough for him to feel it with that light touch.

"Good." He grinned up at her. "You like that idea."

"Not tonight?" she questioned, looking down to see his cock twitch eagerly. *He likes the idea as much as I do.* She had to admit, it was nice to have the evidence of his interest on display.

"We aim to find what you enjoy. Not what I want."

"But I like that idea."

"And I like it too much. I wish to make this last."

He stood and she was only a little disappointed. He tilted his head at the bed. She took the suggestion as wise; after all, her knees were becoming most unreliable.

She moved away from him towards the bed and then paused, feeling impish.

"It's so very high."

He gave a low chuckle and came over swiftly, kneeling to offer her his cupped hands. She placed one stockinged foot in and he tossed her easily into the very center of the bed.

She giggled, actually giggled! Then dampened that inclination and arranged herself as her other husbands had expected – on her back, legs wide, passive.

Still kneeling beside the bed, he looked up at her

prostrate form, and then stood in that fluid way of his. He claimed to be clumsy, but she thought he was quite the opposite. Or perhaps it was simply that his grace was all expended here, in the bedchamber.

She expected him to cast himself atop her and take her then. From the glassy sheen of desire in his eyes, it was what he wanted. It must be. To plunder.

But when she put her arms up and open to receive him, he shook his head and remained standing.

"Nay, lass. Remember, I am no taker."

"Oh."

He reached over, powerful arm muscles coiled as he arranged her a little upright with the pillows tucked underneath, solicitous, as if she were ill.

"Why?"

"So you can watch me."

"Oh, dear." Preshea wasn't certain she wanted such intimacy. The anticipation, too, was risky. Never before had anyone taken so long with her, for any reason. It was gratifying... and frightening. For there, under all his care, was the certain knowledge of what he really wanted from her.

"You want me to lose control."

"In pleasure. Yes."

"That would require trust."

"And you dinna trust anyone."

She stared with wide eyes as he walked to the foot of the bed and sat on the counterpane, scooting close to her. He picked up one stockinged foot and began to rub it. Her foot began to forget the high-heeled slippers of earlier that night. It felt so good, she gave a little "oh" of delight.

"I don't trust anyone enough for that."

"Aye. A sadness, that. So, I work for your pleasure tonight, your trust later."

There he goes again, assuming there will be a later.

Preshea could not deny that she was wildly curious. Desperate to know what he might do next. So far, it had all been so warm and wonderful. So, she let herself trust him, with her body at least. For this one night.

He moved to the other foot, and then began to work his way up her leg. First with hands and then with his lips. Through her silk stockings, his touch made her skin feel tight and sensitive. His lips were feather soft, broken by the occasional brush of teeth, the flick of a tongue, until eventually he had worked his way up to the tops of her stockings. There, the white flesh of her thighs quivered under his mouth. And he would keep moving up.

"No! You said tomorrow."

He laughed then. "I said *standing* tomorrow. Tonight, lie back. Watch."

He dipped down between her legs, nuzzling against her. She protested, embarrassed that he would want to do such a scandalous thing. Until that moment, Preshea had thought she was the most scandalous person she knew. Now she was beginning to think this self-effacing Scotsman had hidden depths. And, as it turned out, hidden skills.

He was insistent, although never rough or brutal about it. He coaxed her thighs apart with soothing hands, and eventually she relaxed because, she had to admit, it was a glorious feeling. Tingly. Like just before a sneeze, only better and, of course, situated somewhat lower down.

His tongue was remarkable, coiling and uncoiling. She wondered, somewhat hysterically, if the burr of Scottish brogue made a man's tongue more flexible. He nibbled to one side and the other, then licked flat fully across. She jerked at the intensity of the sensation and found herself writhing. *Ladies of quality do not writhe!*

He paused, hand to her belly, holding her still, blue eyes glazed with lust.

"Sit up, please." Preshea was shocked to find her voice shaking, her control slipping.

His eyes pleaded.

She gave him the reassurance he craved. "Not to stop. Just for a moment. I want to see you. I need to know you are enjoying this, too. Please."

He did as she asked, rocking back and rising onto his heels.

Remarkable. He was quite certainly enjoying this.

"Very well." Preshea corrected the tremor in her voice, remembering those hours of elocution lessons. *One must always take the greatest care with one's words.* Years it had taken to fix her childhood lisp. "Proceed."

Relief and need flooded his face. She noticed that something else swelled in response to her order. Did he like the command in her voice? *Fascinating.*

He dove back in, barely pausing to breathe. His tongue devilish and driving. Urging her along. She didn't know what crescendo she was heading towards, but she'd decided to give him her body, and he seemed rather good at playing it. *As though I were some violin and his tongue the bow.*

He swiped across her again. The tingling was unrelenting now, almost painful with intensity. Spikes of pleasure arrowed through her.

He pressed against her more firmly, tongue insistent. He would not be denied, whatever the ending of this symphony.

He slid a single finger inside her and she started. But it felt so good to be filled. Better than good – superb. So much better than the dry, tearing stretch of her husbands' pathetic efforts.

Once more, his tongue swiped and pressed. Then the tingling exploded and she was soaring. Splintering and fracturing and spinning as if drunk on champagne *and* dancing a waltz *and* perfectly executing a killing blow… all at the same time.

Only when she went to speak did Preshea realize she was biting her hand to keep back the sounds. "Holy smokes."

She felt his rumble of amusement against her legs. His cheek rested on her thigh and he was kissing her softly there. He had removed his finger but kept his hand pressed against her throbbing core.

Eventually, he looked up. His face was wet with her juices and his eyes were still glazed.

"You can't like that," Preshea was embarrassed enough to protest.

His eyes cleared and he quirked one eyebrow. Then he reared back, coming to his knees between her thighs. He evidently had liked it. His cock was huge and hard with a little moisture at the tip.

Fear struck her then. Would he take her now, drive into her with no thought but for his own satisfaction?

He did not fall upon her; instead he sat back on his heels and reached down for her hands, pulling her up to her own knees. He wrapped her in a strong, soothing hug. Not too confining. She was appalled by how much she loved it, melted into him.

He kissed her then. His mouth musky and salty with her flavor. She realized it was the first time he had kissed her lips. It turned carnal, all tongue and teeth. She shifted forward, wrapping as much of herself as she could about his broad, muscled body, rubbing her stomach against his hardness, surprised at her own eagerness.

She could feel the surge of his back muscles under her arms as he twisted away from her. She thought he was breaking free, rejecting her enthusiasm, but then she found herself carried up and over, landing sprawled atop him.

Frustrated, she banged his chest with a tiny fist. "What now? Get on with it!"

He laughed then, fully laughed, vibrating under her hands.

"Ride me."

"What?"

"You. Ride. Me. That way, you're in control."

"I can do that?"

"I suspect you will be quite good at it."

"My stockings are still on," she said, as if that

were some kind of objection.

"Oh, aye."

"You like that?"

"Aye." He actually blushed a bit at that. Given all the things they had done, she wasn't sure he could blush. It was adorable.

It was also another touch of power – she still had clothing on, he did not. And he liked it more than he cared to admit.

She took her time, partly to see if she liked the sensation and partly because her caution seemed to drive him mad. He held himself so still, but she could see that it cost him, sweat beading his forehead, neck corded with tension, jaw stiff. Surely, he wanted to thrust into her. But no. He let her sink onto him slowly and set the pace.

Which she did.

It was not unlike horse riding. Although, she fancied she was better at this than the canter. And it was certainly much more enjoyable.

She found that if she swiveled her hips in exactly the right way, she could chase the tingling sensation again. So she did, moving as she liked.

He lay under her, watching, suffering (for surely he was desperate for release), but also smug with her pleasure. He arched against her out of instinct, all coiled need bent to her will.

"Touch me again?" she asked.

He did, gliding his hands up her ribcage and breasts before pinching her nipples, as if he knew that was what she really wanted.

Preshea was fracturing again, spinning out and

around. Not quite so far as the first, but still there, still flying.

She lost the rhythm, collapsing down. He grabbed her hips to keep the pace, slow but steady.

It still felt good.

"Preshea, lass," his eyes begged, voice quivering, "May I?"

She hated to say it, him having given so much, but it was a truth that needed saying. "Children would complicate matters."

"I understand."

He bucked under her then, holding her hips to keep her against him. Guiding her but even now, not too rough, careful of his strength. Not clumsy with it. He was never clumsy. She enjoyed watching him lose control beneath her. The tingles started again, although she hadn't the energy to pursue them, and she did not think he had the will to hold out long enough for her to try. Although, knowing him, he'd do his damnedest if she asked.

He lifted her off him at the last, seating her back onto his thighs. Care for her safety even as, face contorted, he spilled onto his own stomach and chest.

It was incredibly erotic to watch and left him looking utterly vulnerable.

I could kill him so easily right now, Preshea thought.

He was boneless under her, entirely at her mercy. She felt it, too (the profound relief after pleasure) but she was also energized.

"You do realize I could end you now with so little effort?"

"Are you certain you've had full use of me, lass? You wouldna wish to waste resources."

"Quite right. Maybe later."

"I'd as lief you dinna."

Preshea found she'd rather not either.

Which really was a concern. Always, there was a tiny part of her that wanted to kill any man she knew. On principle. With Gavin, as easy as it would be to accomplish, she had not the slightest inclination. That terrified her.

In Preshea's world, the man she didn't want to kill was as near to a man she might love as made no difference.

CHAPTER NINE

The Deadlier of the Species

Her absence woke him.

He had not been sleeping, only dozing, but the weight of her against him was such a comfort that the lack caused him to sit up.

Preshea was standing at the window, naked. The fire still blazed (he had made certain to build it up), so she likely felt no cold.

She looked ethereal and bereft.

"It's all right to have enjoyed yourself, lass." He tried to fix the loneliness in her stance with words.

She turned to face him, her arms crossed protectively over her breasts. Was she guarding herself from him or from her own thoughts? Her face, for once, was mobile with confusion and not at all haughty.

He did not approach and take her in his arms,

although he ached to do so. It wouldn't work. It wasn't the right tactic. He wondered if she guessed that one of his roles within the Coldsteam Guards had been that of master tactician.

He said, very softly, "Who did this to you?"

She raised an eyebrow at him.

"Nay, lass. Who made you so wary of men?"

"My father." Her faced stilled, no confusion there.

"Was he violent?"

"Not really. He was proud of my beauty, in a strange way. He didn't want to damage the goods." Her tone was very flat, her words chosen with exacting care.

"So, just cruel?"

"Yes, just that. He liked to wound with words. Taught me to do the same, I suppose. He was particularly adept at unfounded accusations. I sometimes think it might have been easier if he had yelled at me for being what I already was. He wasn't one to identify a weakness and play upon it. That would require too much effort, learning about another person."

She paused, formulating her words so as not to wound, he supposed. She had to think carefully when speaking truth, his lass. "There was a footman. He was older, kind to me, fatherly. Used to carry me piggyback about the house."

Gavin's skin prickled and he focused on making himself calm, trying to be as unthreatening as possible. Not easy in a man his size. Although nudity helped.

"What happened?" He needed some reality of her life, of her past, that was nothing to do with the artificial aristocrat she presented to society. Yet his need was hurting her, and that was nigh unbearable. Perhaps he should let her slide back into truncated words and false expressions.

But she was gracious, gave him more of her ugliness. "Father accused him, accused us, of all manner of things. Sexual things. I was ten. I understood little except that it was not true, and disgusting. Father explained it all to me in detail. Then I understood too much. I vomited in Father's best slippers. The footman was horsewhipped and dismissed without a character. All because he was kind to me."

"So, you learned kindness as weakness."

"Is it not? Well" —she gave a tiny smile— "perhaps not for you."

He would not let her be distracted. "What happened after?"

"He sent me to finishing school. Not the normal kind. We were taught other things. Etiquette, of course. But there are spaces in between *the done thing* and *the right phrase*. Spaces where a lady may hide information or death."

"And your father?"

"I remember returning home that first Christmas. Already, I knew what I could achieve. He sent me away to learn espionage and assassination, to become a weapon for his use. He never once considered that I would have my own plans."

"Did you kill him, Preshea?"

"No. But I did poison him. Not enough. A little cyanide here and there. Every time I was home. Once, I put foxglove in his minced veal simply to watch his heart race away from him, there at the dinner table. Then, the final year, I let him catch me at it." She rubbed her hands up and down her arms. "His face was so shocked, demanding an explanation. As if, by right of blood, I was the betrayer for knowing he was against me. I reminded him that he had sent me to that school. He knew the curriculum."

Gavin stayed frozen, waiting.

She spoke, each word an arrow aimed to hit a mark. "I told him that when I was home, he would never be safe. I reminded him of how many household items are deadly, and that I knew them all." She moved to the fireplace, looking into the flames instead of at him. Her face, in profile, was marble. "Did you know that even wood ash from a fire, mixed with water, can be poison?"

Gavin shook his head.

She gave a tiny grimace, fracturing the marble. "I can't forget his face. He was very handsome. But he wasn't at that moment. He was so scared. I" —her voice splintered— "I enjoyed that. So, I told him about phossy jaw. Did you know radium is disfiguring and difficult to detect? My father's greatest fear, I think – ugliness. I gave him two options. He could have me committed to an insane asylum or he could marry me off. The first would be embarrassing, the second lucrative. Of course, he chose marriage. Although I did say I could not guarantee my husband's safety. I advised him to choose wisely. You see, I'm not a kind person."

Gavin shifted to sit more upright, careful with his movements. She didn't want his kindness; the best he could give her right now was his attention. "Did he?"

"Did he what?"

"Choose wisely?"

Preshea slumped, sinking down into a chair. Still graceful, but she looked not so much ethereal as frail. He ached to go to her. *Not yet.*

"Not really. My first husband could be quite brutal. Especially in his cups." She gestured to her body. "It was a good change. Well, not good exactly, but at least different after seventeen years."

Gavin felt his gut coil and surge with bile. He couldn't stand the thought of her hurting, not the tiniest bit of it. Not his Preshea, not this pristine weapon of a woman.

She kept talking as if driven by his disgust. "I believe that he, too, was proud of my looks. Never touched my face. Mostly pinching – upper arms, ribs. Did you know that if you twist your fingers just so, the bruise is heart-shaped? He died, one dose for each heart he gave me."

Gavin felt almost as though he could taste her revenge, feel it for her. He wanted more than that.

She saw the question in his face. "He died." Her tone was final. "Please don't ask me how exactly. The others died too. Naturally, not so naturally, what does it matter? They were all arranged for me. My father might think he chose, but he did not. I did my duty under the terms of my indenture. You're a soldier, you know what it is to follow orders, to do what you are told."

"Aye, lass, I do at that. Even the unpleasant stuff." Gavin was not feeling so casual as he appeared. In fact, he was finding it difficult to breathe, listening to her speak of the men who had come before him.

"And the next one?" If she were in a forthcoming mood, he wouldn't stop her. Even if it kept her across the room, half a mile away. Gavin didn't know why he wanted to know about the infamous husbands of Lady Preshea Villentia so badly. Perhaps because it was insight into her.

Slowly, carefully, then faster, she began to tell him about the others. The second: "Not particularly capable, and resentful of me because of it. Liked to yell a lot, he did, spilled all his secrets that way."

She talked of them flatly, her words ice crystals of clear, perfect misery. It was the voice she used when she wanted nothing to show. Each phrase assassinated by its own punctuation.

"He did nothing to me physically, nothing at all. Turns out he had... other preferences."

Gavin tried for sympathy. "Men?"

"Children."

Gavin could not hide his repulsion.

"Exactly." She noted his expression with approval. "Hard to regret, that one." A pause. "Richard was third. He was fine, a tradesman. Liked me as a status symbol. Left me to myself and wasn't mean with my allowance. We rattled along well enough. He kept out of my business. I kept out of his. In fact, after a single unsatisfying bedroom encounter, he ignored me. Perhaps that's worse?"

Gavin felt nothing but anger for these husbands of hers. He was not jealous at all, just sad, and sorry for her, and ashamed of himself and his sex.

"What happened to him, then, if you weren't... If he wasn't intended..." Gavin struggled for the correct words. He was a forthright man, a soldier; espionage was not a comfortable place.

"Died in a carriage accident with his mistress. Six months after our wedding."

He blinked, surprised at the blatancy of the statement.

"Oh" —she grinned— "it wasn't a secret. It also wasn't my doing. Not my style. I suspect it was arranged, though. Pity about the girl."

She paused, frowning. Remembering to feel concern for someone she never knew, or simply gathering her thoughts?

"Last was Alfred – Viscount Villentia." She gestured to herself as if to say *as you see me now*. "I was twenty-four when we married. He was seventy-six."

"God's breath!" Gavin couldn't stop the exclamation.

"I actually liked him. He didn't want anything from me. He was too old and not all there up top, you see? Utterly harmless. I treated him the best I knew how."

She glared at him then, as if accusing him of wrecking something. As if his offering her anything, even the pleasure of one glorious night together, were an insult. To what? That last sham of a marriage? The shams of all her previous marriages?

"Lass, I dinna kiss you to stop you from talking. I dinna need to smother you to prove anything to myself or any man."

She stood and came back towards him, but she was different now. Poised.

He felt a wrenching ache. She was closing herself off, slipping away, not telling him something important.

She stopped next to the bed. It was exactly the right height for her to look down on him.

"My life is what I wanted, don't you see? I used to brag about it in school. How wonderful to be a widow. Widows have autonomy. Widows with money and a title have *lots* of autonomy. I got scandal and fear alongside. So, I am free. Well, free enough."

She held herself perfectly still, as one will in bathwater that is too hot, for any movement might cause pain. It was the way some of his youngest officers held themselves after battle. The ones who should never have gone to war, the ones who were too young, or too kind, or too romantic for all the blood. The ones who would return home broken.

"Who are you, Gavin Ruthven, to dare try and take that from me?"

Her focused stillness was that of some fractured vase held together with wax. Gavin felt a profound pity, and he knew she would hate him for it. So, he held himself equally still, afraid to say anything. Afraid to touch her, although she was within reach, for she might shatter as easily as she might melt against him.

Her eyes were hard. Eyes he knew were madder

blue, although, in the half-light, he couldn't see the color.

"Why should you try to change what I have become? What I have arranged for myself? It's enough. It's what I want. It's what I have always wanted."

"Lass, I dinna want you changed. I only want you here. Come back to bed." He judged it safe to ask – her wistful loneliness had turned to anger. She was focused on him now and not the past.

Too focused, as it turned out.

"It's too much. You're too much. This" —her gesture encompassed the room, the well used sheets, and him— "it isn't for me. Find some *lass* who isn't shaped to be deadly. I've nothing left for you. He already took it."

She might be referring to her father, or her husbands, or the mysterious patron who once held her indenture.

She gathered up her clothing – careful to leave nothing behind. She departed his room with equal care, still naked but for her stockings.

Gavin did not worry for her. She knew full well how to move around a house without being seen. He worried for himself. What strategy now? He would not force her into anything. Could not.

He sank into the warmth of the big bed and ached for her small form next to his. He hurt for her, because he suspected she could not. For what she had chosen to do and what had been done to her. All the men who had come before him had molded her with touches that even his big hands, and all the kindness behind them, couldn't wipe away. Was it possible to give her enough to fill the void left by what others had taken?

The next day, the rain returned. Preshea felt it suited her mood admirably.

Gavin watched her, and though she hated herself for it, she watched Gavin.

She had done the correct thing. *Did it have to hurt this much?* Other necessary actions hadn't hurt; why should this one be so painful?

The rain brought with it a house-wide melancholy. The party sat about the drawing room, slumped under grey light.

Preshea wasn't certain what drove her to do it, but she revealed some of her inner turmoil to Miss Pagril and Lady Flo.

Lady Flo embroidered while Miss Pagril flipped through a book of fashion, pausing to comment on some outrageous dress or another.

"Even I," said Preshea at one, "would look bilious in that monstrosity."

"Goodness, everyone seems out of temper today. Even you, Lady Villentia." Miss Pagril was disposed to be less harsh about the gown in question.

"Do I? I had better keep sterner control of my expressions."

"Must you always be so reserved?" Miss Pagril was genuinely curious.

"It is better, I find, to give few openings to others."

"Not even to the good captain?"

Preshea turned to where the other girl gestured.

Gavin was looking at them while Mr Jackson took his turn at cards.

"His focus is on you, Lady Villentia, not us. In case you were in any doubt." Miss Pagril attempted a tease.

Before last night, Preshea might have bristled, but now she knew the truth. Firstly, that the full force of the captain's attention, and affection, was indeed on her. Secondly, that Miss Pagril would not welcome his courtship, should he try.

Still, the young girl's comment was a tad familiar for Preshea's taste, so she made her tone short. "I did not wonder."

Lady Flo's face fell, but she did not stop embroidering. "You do not welcome his interest?"

"No more than you or Miss Pagril might. Although" —she paused significantly— "for different reasons."

Lady Flo gasped.

Miss Pagril turned a piercing look on Preshea. "I'm sure I have *no* idea what you are implying."

Preshea was moved to be cruel; *no one* bare-faced her into verbal surrender. "Oh, I think you do. Next time you relocate late at night, may I suggest you leave the candle behind?"

"Oh!" Lady Flo dropped her tambour and put a hand to her mouth, crimson with humiliation.

Miss Pagril's eyes narrowed. "What do you intend to do?"

Preshea sighed. She had always known she was

bad at female friendships. She seemed unable to stop herself from sabotaging them. "Do? Nothing."

"What do you want from us to keep silent?" Miss Pagril's tone was forcibly casual, her implication insulting.

Preshea's lip curled. "I'm *not* interested in blackmailing children. You've nothing to offer me that I could possibly want. You mistake my meaning. I merely wish to encourage caution. If you insist on reckless behavior, don't be stupid about it."

"How kind." Miss Pagril's voice was icy.

Lady Flo picked up her embroidery, face now white. "Jane, don't."

"I take it you approve, then?" Miss Pagril was made of sterner stuff.

The girl was asking for Preshea's thoughts on aberrant sexual choices. Preshea, to be honest, had none. She'd never been asked to use her wiles on another woman, and did not feel the inclination herself. Since the matter had no bearing on her, personally or professionally, she'd given it no thought at all. But she refused to sanction the bumbling of an amateur sneak, so she willfully misinterpreted the question.

"Certainly not. Your form is terrible. Your execution atrocious. I could hear your footfalls before I even topped the stairs."

Lady Blingchester joined them at that moment. "To what are you referring, Lady Villentia? Is that criticism I hear?"

Without pause, Preshea said smoothly, "Miss Pagril's form at the waltz. Very poor."

Lady Blingchester sniffed. "Well, of course it is – she's not permitted the waltz! Too risqué. But how should you know to comment?"

"I saw the young ladies waltzing together down the hallway the other evening. Really, Your Grace, Lady Blingchester, your girls may not be *allowed* to waltz, but I assure you the dance is here to stay. They should at least know how to do it gracefully, in case of emergency."

The Duchess of Snodgrove had joined the conversation. "Waltz emergency?"

"We are in safe quarters here – perhaps a lesson?" Preshea was nothing if not a mistress of diversion.

The duchess flipped open her fan and fluttered it about. "Oh, I don't think…"

Preshea smiled. "I shall demonstrate, if one of the gentlemen would oblidge me? The two young ladies may dance with each other and Lady Violet with her brother. Thus, no impropriety could possibly occur. If Miss Leeton would honor us with a tune?"

Although the chaperones clucked in mild disapproval, the young people seemed to find dancing a wonderful idea (anything to relieve the monotony). The furniture was pushed back.

"I will help demonstrate, Lady Villentia." Mr Jackson bounced forward.

Gavin stopped him. "You're a gruesome waltzer, lad. Think on the corruption inherent in your example."

Mr Jackson laughed, not at all upset by the criticism. Since his ladylove was off limits in this endeavor, he allowed the truth in Gavin's words. "Go on, then, Ruthven. Don't let him fool you, Lady Villentia. He's a pirouetting fool, for all he looks like a water buffalo."

Gavin snorted, not unlike said buffalo, and scooped Preshea into waltz position.

Until that moment, Preshea hadn't understood how intimate the waltz really was. In Gavin's arms, she finally comprehended the fuss. She was surrounded by his warmth, steadied under his massive hands, forced to look into his blue eyes.

Lord Lionel took Lady Violet into his arms, joking in a brotherly way. The two young ladies, after some debate, settled on Miss Pagril leading and Lady Flo following. Preshea wondered if this was representative of any other aspect of their relationship.

Miss Leeton plunked out a waltz. Preshea called instructions while Gavin demonstrated the steps. It was a simple dance and Jack had not overblown his friend's abilities. Gavin was an excellent partner.

The others picked it up easily. It was a sedate affair with the eyes of all fixed upon them.

Preshea was brutally aware of the feel of Gavin's hand through the clothing at her back. Of the smell of him – musky and spicy and male. Not threatening. Even with his size, she felt no fear. He held her comfortably, supportive, with no attempt to pull her closer than the prescribed distance, offering only guidance as they swirled about the small space.

Would he partner in all things like this? Preshea coldly stopped herself from that line of thinking. She had exposed her past to him last night so he would understand her choices. She hoped to prevent his falling in love with her. Foolishly, she had once told herself that she ought to break his heart. Now it was the last thing she wanted. She owed him something for showing her that passion between a man and a woman could be good and decent. She intended to pay him back by leaving him alone, and leaving him as intact as possible.

He would not be allowed to love her. Not if she had anything to do with it.

Lady Flo and Miss Pagril wafted by, casting frightened glances in her direction. Silly chits. Neither of them had thought to ask why Preshea had been outside her *own* room last night. Preshea had admitted to seeing Miss Pagril enter Lady Flo's bedchamber, so she too must have been roaming. *Lord save me from innocent girls with no professional training!*

"So, there you have it. The waltz." Preshea concluded the dance lesson. "Not so bad, is it?"

"Most refreshing to undertake a bit of exercise. Shall we continue?" Lord Lionel was puffing slightly, rosy-cheeked but enjoying himself, for all he partnered his sister.

What had begun as a ploy became a pleasant afternoon of light exercise. The Blingchesters even joined for a quadrille.

Once the waltz was retired for more acceptable fare, Gavin danced with every lady there, including Lady Blingchester and the Duchess of Snodgrove. So did Mr Jackson, although perhaps not so gracefully.

They ended on another waltz, Miss Leeton having started it unasked. *Cheeky lady.*

Gavin took Preshea back into his arms. As had already been established, she was his only option for the waltz.

"We dance verra well together." It was not dancing to which he referred.

"We do, but the music will stop soon."

"That doesna mean we should end our partnership prematurely."

Saucy blighter. "True. But you know the rules of society as well as I – you may not ask for another."

"Na unless we are engaged."

"Don't." Her steps stuttered.

He stopped that tactic instantly. "I'll never ask for more than you're prepared to give, Lady Villentia. Never. I hope you know that by now."

"Yes. I believe I do."

"Perhaps you could see yourself taking another spin about the room, later tonight?"

"Perhaps."

Gavin wasn't certain she would come to him again. He was fairly certain sure she wanted to, but not that she would allow herself the indulgence.

Still, he made sure everything was ready for her. The fire built up, the counterpane turned back. He'd washed thoroughly, and had Mawkins give him an evening pass with the razor, much to his valet's surprise and annoyance.

"What need have you for a shave so late? You aren't going to a ball. Have you gone mad?"

Gavin glared. "Dinna trouble yourself with reasoning – 'tis not healthy in a valet."

With a long-suffering sigh, Mawkins retrieved the shaving things. "You're getting quirky in your old age, sir. Don't know how long I can take *quirky*." Mawkins was eyeing the banyan with displeasure. Mawkins wasn't Scottish. He must be forgiven his poor taste.

Gavin, of course, suspected his valet knew exactly why he might wish a shave before bed.

Gavin had not lied to Preshea. He was discreet and careful about his liaisons. He had entertained only two ladies since resigning his commission. Mawkins hadn't known of either. In the past, the valet always shaved Gavin without comment before Gavin left to attend private evening arrangements. But that had been in London; he might well have been going to his club as going to his mistress.

Mawkins' annoyance, no doubt, stemmed from his not knowing which young lady had curried Gavin's favor. *What,* Gavin wondered, *are the betting odds belowstairs?*

"Do you require the claret, sir?"

"Aye. Two glasses, please."

Mawkins bowed stiffly, in a manner that suggested he was gravely put out with Gavin's keeping secrets. Still, he never shirked his duties, returning promptly with the claret. He took away the last of Gavin's garments to be pressed with only an exasperated look.

So Gavin waited, clean-shaven, and hoped.

Bonnie lass, she did come. Slipping into his room

so quickly, he might not have noticed had he not been staring at the door, willing it to open.

She'd changed into a dressing gown. Gavin was a little disappointed, for he liked the titillation of undressing a woman one layer at a time. However, it was a beautiful silky thing that draped about her in rivers of white fabric.

She moved across his chamber with a confidence she hadn't shown the previous night.

He couldn't stop the grin. He had given her that at least – a boldness within lust. He could tell from the way she walked that she intended to claim him. He was delighted to let her.

Having just tended the fire, he stood clutching the poker in one hand like a clumsy gyte. He put it back in its cradle, bashful.

"I could grow to both love and hate this thing." She fingered the shawl collar of his banyan.

"Why's that, lass?"

"It's quite the eyesore, but it does fit you beautifully, and it is easy to remove."

Suiting her actions to words, she stripped him of the offending article. Unashamed, he held out his arms so she could pull it off easily.

She ran her fingers over him. Her hands were stronger than one might expect. His breath quickened. She was rushing, pulling him along with her, and he was powerless to resist.

It was sublime.

She pressed against him, all silk-covered flesh, rubbing like a cat. She stroked him everywhere, over his chest and back, down lower, squeezing both in front and behind. He jerked in her grasp but let her do whatever she wished – touch whatever she liked.

She wasn't speaking this time. She was happy to explore without asking and he was happy to let her. He need not give her permission; she already had that. She had all of him, anytime she liked.

Turning words into mere sounds was easier anyway. Small gasps and moans could not be confessions. There was nothing to deny or avoid. She would not run if he offered her his body; she would if he offered his heart.

So, he converted *I love you* to tiny kisses. And *I will treasure you forever* into long caresses of the kind that made her undulate against him.

It seemed to work.

She stepped back, lovely in her confidence. Untying and dropping her dressing gown, she stood before him in nothing but her hair, long and loose about her.

He waited. His interest evident. Her gaze was drawn there. Her eyes dilated. He would wait like this forever if she wished it of him. He would be the proof she needed of a different kind of man. In the end, she was likely to ignore it, but he had to hope she was strong enough to accept. She was strong enough to have come back to him tonight, although he'd have wagered against himself in Mawkins' pool. She'd been so confident in her denial when she left his bed, and so cold all day. He thought he'd lost her. The relief at having her back was nigh overwhelming.

"You said to ask you again tonight." She spoke at last. Her voice was still clipped, not yet roughened by desire or tears. The moisture he felt was in his own eyes, not hers.

He let his head fall forward, for he did not want her to see his sentiment. She might discard him for it. Preshea admired strength, not empathy. It made him self-conscious. "I did?"

"Yes."

"About what?"

"About what *you* wanted."

He relaxed. This was easy territory. He wasn't afraid to open himself up to her in that way. After all, how much more lost could he be to her? She already had all the ammunition she needed to destroy him, whether she knew it or not. "You hadna guessed?"

"No. Well, perhaps a little."

He blushed, actually blushed. "I want to please you."

"What?"

"Ah." He cleared his throat. Considering all that they had done and said the last night, she obviously found it amusing to see him embarrassed. "For me, it is about your pleasure. I dinna know the right way of saying it, but I wish it to be for you. This, me, everything." He gestured down towards his arousal, up towards his heart and head, struggling to explain. "I dinna enjoy it if the woman is unwilling. I canna function if she's under sufferance or passive. I dinna believe it makes me less a man, although my peers might disagree. Fortunately, they are na privy to my proclivities."

Preshea cocked her head, frowning. Her hands, thank heavens, never stopped moving – caressing, testing the weight and heat of him. She clearly enjoyed touching him and took reassurance in it. "Does that mean you wish me to be in charge, give orders? As though you were a servant?"

"If you like. I wouldna protest. Ideally, I should wish for plenty of time to learn what makes you moan, what makes you wet. I'd as lief please you without your having to ask, although I'm happy to take requests."

She seemed to come to some decision, then she nodded. "If I am demanding, I always get exactly what I wish for from the milliner, and the dressmaker, and the cobbler, and so forth. Why should this be any different?"

He strained to hide a smile. "Why indeed? I'm thinking if we move to the bed, I might start taking measurements?"

CHAPTER TEN

A Scotsman Without His Beard

Preshea was going to say that, from last night's endeavors, she already had his measure. Then she noticed something peculiar about his bed.

He had tied a cravat to each of the posts. It reminded Preshea of something she'd once learned, on the securing of prisoners for interrogation.

"I will not!" She revealed herself and her fear immediately in a way she would have thought impossible a few days before. "How could you ask?"

He rested a hand on her shoulder, gentling her like a skittish horse. "Softly, lass. Those are na for you. They are for me."

"What?"

"You are a lass who prefers control. I'm thinking that in this way, you'd see me as no threat. Simply yours for the taking."

She tilted her head. "For the asking?" she corrected, not liking the aggression in the word.

"That, I already am."

Preshea was surprised to find how excited she was by the idea. This big man, entirely at her mercy, with no ability to act on his own needs. "You would do this thing voluntarily?"

"With pleasure."

She did not use the knots she'd been taught (the ones that limited blood flow, designed to be cruel). She tied him firmly, but in a pretty bow. That way he could, with a little dexterity, pull the tail and be free without her aid.

He lay spread before her and under her gaze – passive, eager, and uninhibited. As if he had waited for this all along. She did not wish to think of him as different, but there seemed no way around it.

Preshea explored at her leisure. She used her hands mainly and her teeth a little to nip here or there. She applied lips and tongue sparingly, unsure but eager. She found herself delighted by his noises. *How close the sounds of pleasure are to those of pain.*

She crawled over him on her quest, not concerned about her weight, so slight compared to his.

She adored that she could watch and see if what she did appealed. There was obvious evidence when she aroused him. He enjoyed the licks a great deal, her use of teeth slightly less so. Depending on how she moved, what he could see of her body also caused a reaction. She found herself playing him like an instrument, to see the way he jerked and moaned, the moisture beading at the tip of his cock.

"Lass," he said. "You're killing me here."

"Now, now, I promise things would feel a great deal different if death were in play." She was straddling him, faced towards his feet, exploring the length and texture of him with long, tight strokes.

"Just a taste, please?"

Again, she was amazed that he would want such a thing. But his eagerness was genuine, for when she backed up and over his face, he strained his neck up to taste her, using that wicked tongue exactly as he had previously to drive and torture her. She ground against him without thinking, chasing the tingling sensation, and he drove her towards it. He struggled against the ties as if he dearly wished to touch her, to hold her against his mouth. When the explosion came, it surprised her with its suddenness and intensity. She had been so delighted with her explorations, she had not realized how aroused she was.

She moved off and turned, collapsing back against the pillows, feeling wet and replete.

"You shaved. It's nicer, less prickly."

He turned to look at her, eyes heavy-lidded. "My valet couldna countenance the request."

Oh, dear lord. "He knows!"

"He's no snitch, and he's no notion which lass I might be entertaining." He paused. "Or lad, I suppose it could be. He's sour with ignorance."

Preshea let out a relieved sigh. "Oh, well, then, if you'd risk a hanging offense simply to divert attention from me…"

"Dinna think as I'd go that far, *leannan sìth*."

She was inspired to be devilish and twist his

meaning. "You're ashamed of me as a lover, keeping me secret from your valet?"

"Daft lassie. You've a reputation to protect. One that doesna, so far as I've heard, include being one of *those* widows."

"No, I'm considered too dangerous for dalliance. Except by foolish Highland captains."

"Exactly so. Now, am I risking much if I ask to be untied?"

She evaluated him. He was still fully aroused and no doubt eager to seek his own satisfaction.

She was not averse. But she was not willing, just yet, to cede control either.

"No, I like you captive."

He gave a plaintive wiggle. Which caused certain parts of him to flop about in a ridiculous and highly unthreatening manner.

"I've plans, sir," she instructed, tone severe.

He brightened. "Aye? Weel, I'm at your mercy, then."

He was indeed. Preshea elected to take ruthless advantage of that fact.

She rode him again, the ties allowing her to set the pace with little influence from him, although he was straining and growling near the end and the bed frame was creaking in a most alarming manner. It was wonderful, all that coiled muscle vibrating under her with nowhere to go, and no means of release except what she permitted.

In the end, she dismounted and used her hands; far gone into lust though she might be, children, as she had said before, would be a liability. She found she enjoyed watching him spend himself to her will, at her dictate, under her touch.

Afterwards, she untied him. Feeling warm with release and delight and flushed pride at her new skills. She was also disconcerted by her decision to return to his bed. She'd no excuse for loving him a second time. *So, why did I?*

Preshea Villentia refused to lie to herself. To others, all the time. To herself, never.

I wanted him. Simple as that. And he made it plain he was available to my desire. Already I want him again. And I will want him tomorrow. And the night after.

But the house party would end, and they would go their separate ways, and she would never see him again unless she chose. And he would never see her again unless she chose, because disappearing was also one of her skills.

She left the bed, reaching for her dressing gown. "So, tomorrow night?" *I'm weak in the face of massive Scotsmen. Or at least this one.*

"I'm na giving over my banyan, lass."

She met his mock seriousness with her own. Good, tonight they would not talk about matters of the past or the heart.

"As if I would ask such a thing. Although I am glad you gave over the beard."

"Mawkins will be suspicious."

"I suggest you shave before supper. Perhaps that will allay his concerns."

"You're a devious creature."

"You have no idea."

"You secured the house before you came to me?" He reached for her hand, dangling at her side, and stroked her wrist with his callused thumb.

"Of course. Formerly Connie sends her regards. I believe she has a *tendre* for you."

"Poor lassie, to die so young."

"Still thinks we are engaged, wants to know when we'll be telling her family."

"Aye? When will we?"

"Please don't."

"Lass, I want this clear – I'd apply for the position of fifth husband, if you'd permit."

"Oh, yes? Here I thought you desired a long and happy life."

"Aye, lass, but I'd as soon a shorter one with you than a longer one without."

"Careful what you wish for."

"Lass—"

"No, don't spoil this. Don't make me remind you."

"Remind me of what?"

Preshea took a breath. She had so hoped for a few more nights together. "It's not lies, what they say about me. I've killed, and I was glad to do it, and it was easy. I should do it again if necessary. I'm good at it."

"Dinna think my soldiering was all larking about in foreign lands. I'll wager I'm a better shot with that little revolver than you are, and as like to kill more people with it. What matters that I did it all open-like, under sanction of queen and country? 'Tis still killing. I know how you feel."

"Do you? Do you really? Did you enjoy it?"

He paused, sitting up, rubbing his wrists where the cravats had bit into his flesh. She remembered how he had rubbed her back the night before, to relieve the press of corset lacings. So much care in him, in his touch. "Sometimes, maybe. The heat of battle can be a place of passion, in its way. I was good at killing, too. 'Tis hard to turn aside from a skill at which one excels, no matter how civilization perceives that skill."

Oh, thought Preshea on a moment of wonder, *he does understand.* "But it's *all* I'm good at."

"Now, lass, I'm thinking that's a wee falsehood. What we just did, you're verra good at that."

"Well." Preshea was shocked to feel herself blush. "It's not a skill I should care to market."

"I hope not. What need have you, anyroad?" He seemed quite perplexed.

"You do not feel useless, having resigned your commission? Having given over your only talent?"

"'Tis not my *only* talent, either." He wiggled his eyebrows at her lasciviously.

The conversation was not permitted to continue. Two voices commenced screaming down the hall.

Gavin cursed the interruption. He'd actually been getting somewhere with Preshea. She was not closing him off with her beliefs about herself; the ghosts haunting her words had been silent.

"What the devil!" He grabbed up the poker from

the fire and made for the door.

"Put on your banyan." Her voice interrupted his mad dash. Firm and cool and competent, like that of his major.

Instinctively, the soldier took over and he followed her order.

Preshea peeked out the door while he did so.

"Some kind of dramatic happening in the family wing, outside Lady Flo's room. Oh, dear, I do hope Miss Pagril wasn't even more foolish than last night."

He folded over the front of the banyan. "What's this?"

"They're lovers. You didn't realize?"

Gavin wasn't too surprised. "I saw the intimacy. Didna think it was consummated. That's possible, between women? Remarkable." Gavin considered how such an undertaking might work, thrusting his feet into slippers.

"You're the one with the wicked tongue."

Gavin's imagination soared. "Weel, yes. I take your point. Have you?"

Preshea gave him an exasperated look. "No. But while my own experience is limited, I have benefited somewhat from the expertise of others."

"What?"

"Books, Gavin, dear. I read."

"Oh."

"Now do hurry. I can hardly be the first out of your room, now, can I?"

During the course of the conversation, Preshea had donned her dressing gown and slippers. She pulled back and coiled her hair in such a way that, although dressed *exactly* as she had been when she first entered his room, instead of sensual, she looked demure. It was in the way she held herself, the set of her shoulders, the expression on her face. Truly, his lass was amazing.

"Leave the door ajar when you go."

He marched out, leaving the door behind him slightly open.

Everyone was awake, including a few of the servants.

Gavin strode down the hallway, clutching the poker, and looking as threatening as possible.

The hubbub was indeed centered on Lady Flo's room. The titular occupant was in hysterics on her bed, wrapped in copious blankets.

Miss Pagril was fully dressed, thank heavens, and sitting nearby, clutching Lady Flo's hand and glaring out the window. It was one of those upper rooms that had a large oriel window. It jutted out over the rear garden, providing a most desirable view.

The window was open to the cold night, and looming just outside was the Snodgrove private dirigible. Jack, paralyzed with horror, was half-in and half-out of the thing.

He had a piccolo in one hand and a lobster in the other.

The Duchess of Snodgrove stood near her younger daughter, having a protracted bout of hysterics.

The duke was pacing about – calling for the constabulary, his steward, the local magistrate, his scrivener, the town butcher, his favorite hound, and anyone else he could think of in any position of authority.

Lord and Lady Blingchester hovered in the doorway, eyes avid. "Gone off his crumpet, he has!" said the one to the other.

Lord Lionel was trying to calm his father.

Miss Leeton was tucked into a different corner of the room, clutching a sobbing Lady Violet, patting at her in a consoling manner. The actress's eyes were bright with appreciation for the drama.

Gavin marched in and took control of the situation. Putting his poker to one side, he sent the butler off for smelling salts and sherry.

"Jack! Get yourself and that ridiculous craft out of here. What are you thinking?"

"I only wished to serenade Lady Vi!"

"Chose the wrong window, did you?"

"They're rather difficult to distinguish from the outside when floating."

"Why the piccolo?" Gavin couldn't help but ask.

"It's the only instrument I play."

Gavin tried not to stare at the lobster. He decided not to inquire further. Whatever Jack's reasoning, best to accept that crustaceans were necessary to his view of the world.

"Jack, you daft idiot, shove off." Gavin loved Jack for his easygoing nature and big heart. He was truly the most loyal of friends. But the man could get right barmy notions in his head.

The butler appeared with several glasses of sherry.

Gavin took one for himself and pressed another

on the duke. "Drink that, Your Grace. Do you good."

At this juncture, Preshea appeared. She had on a black velvet robe over her dressing gown. It had a scalloped hem and was collared in fur, making her entirely too regal for a lass who'd recently been writhing with pleasure atop him. Or perhaps that was the source of her regality.

She looked down her nose at everyone. Which she did very nicely, wearing her most *Lady Villentia* face. It was better than a dousing of cold water over the entire company.

"Must you create such a racket? Some of us are trying to sleep. What on earth is going on?" Of course, she knew exactly what was happening; she'd arranged everything. Gavin could see it now – the little hints she dropped in conversation, the way she influenced Jack. Her goal all along, to see his friend make a fool of himself. Not that Jack needed a great deal of help in that regard, but still...

Gavin stared at her in horror.

She caught his expression and her own stuttered. Then, if possible, she became even haughtier.

She turned away from him. "Everyone, do calm down. This is not a crisis. Mr Jackson has made a little mistake in his courtship technique. Perhaps, Lady Violet, this action has convinced you, one way or another?"

"It has certainly convinced me!" cried the Duke of Snodgrove.

Preshea hurried to him and said something in his ear in the guise of lifting a glass of sherry from the tray nearby. He snapped his mouth shut.

She moved to the distraught Lady Violet. The young lady managed to stop sobbing with the aid of the sherry. "Lady Violet?" Preshea pressed.

Gavin didn't want to watch. Why was she bothering? Jack was ruined; she need not nail his coffin closed with her wiles.

"Yes, quite right." Lady Violet hiccoughed.

Preshea chivvied her forward. Gavin wanted to cry at her cruelty. At Jack's poor sad face.

Preshea patted the girl's back gently. Lady Violet raised her head. "Mr Jackson, I'm sorry if anything I've said encouraged you into such rash action. Please understand that I could *never* marry you. You are too bold for someone as timid as I. This kind of behavior, it is too much!"

"But Lady Violet!" Jack cried, impassioned. He tried to step out of the dirigible and through the window. The aircraft bobbed and Jack went flying back into the gondola. The lobster, on the other hand, made it through the window perfectly well and, emboldened by liberty, scuttled under the bed.

Lady Flo, Miss Pagril, and the duchess all shrieked. The duchess jumped onto the bed, joining the younger girls.

Gavin sighed and instructed the footmen to go find a butterfly net, come back, and catch the darned thing.

Lady Violet sucked in a breath and walked to the oriel window. "There is no understanding between us, Mr Jackson. Please accept my decision gracefully."

Jack's head reappeared. He waved the piccolo in distress. "Lady Vi! I beg you."

"No. You are not for me."

"Please."

"You are brash. And... you cannot waltz!"

"You cut me to the very quick!" Jack pressed the piccolo to his forehead.

Gavin winced in empathy and exasperation. *Where did the lad come up with such sentimental blether? I must keep him from reading romantic novels.*

"We *do not* suit. You have no genuine interest in botany!" Lady Violet practically yelled her final conclusion. This was the biggest sin of them all.

Jack hung his head. "That, I cannot deny. Very well, my dear Lady Vi. I shall never recover from this heartbreak, never, but I bow to your wishes." Said bow brought Jack's head into the bowels of the dirigible and out of view.

"Thank heavens. Now, can we all get some sleep?" Preshea would not allow Jack any further dramatic moments.

Of course, it took them considerable time to get the dirigible to float down. No one, not even Jack, could determine how he'd managed to safely fly the darned thing up there. Finally, the helmsman was roused, and through some precarious maneuvering, he attained the gondola and floated Jack to safety.

Everyone else dispersed (except the lobster, who refused to leave the safety of the bed, footmen with butterfly nets notwithstanding). Eventually, Lady Flo said, quite crossly, that so long as he didn't snore, the crustacean might stay until morning. Poor creature, hadn't he too suffered enough for one evening?

"It's a good thing Jane was in your room, Lady Flo, or you should be ruined! A single man at your window like that." Lady Blingchester's tone said she rather hoped for ruination, if only for the delightful scandal.

"Yes, dear, why were you here?" the duchess responded.

Gavin was heading out to find his disgraced friend. He heard Preshea say, "Oh, didn't I hear you talking at dinner, Lady Flo, about a headache? No doubt Miss Pagril was bringing you a restorative."

Poor Preshea, she could not help but meddle.

Jack was eager to leave early the next morning. Without his friend, Gavin had no excuse for staying. The duke was in safe hands with Preshea, and he would report as much to Major Channing. He'd relay what he knew of the rifleman and find out why the werewolf had doubled down on protection. If, indeed, it was he.

Lady Villentia did not wake to see them off. Knowing her assignment was to protect the duke, he must assume her destruction of his friend's prospective engagement was mere spite. He could not deny it hurt. Why bother with such an idiot as Jack? It wasted her talent to be so petty. He was disappointed. Although, sadly, not surprised.

So, Gavin found himself folded into a first class compartment, heading back to London on the morning train. Jack slumped, dejected, opposite.

Gavin was feeling equally dejected and not inclined to talk.

Jack was not so reticent. "I'm all suffering and dashed hopes."

"You brought it on yourself. Why anyone might think a dirigible, a piccolo, and a lobster should advance his suit is beyond me."

"I was desperate. I was losing her favor."

"And with that one act, ensured its absence forever."

"Don't be harsh, Ruthven, old chum. I'm already cut up, tortured by a broken heart."

"Jack, you gyte, a *piccolo*!"

"Do you play?"

"Na my instrument of choice." He thought of Preshea's smooth white skin under his big hands.

"It has a certain peeping wistfulness."

"If you must be daft, I'd as lief you wallowed in silence."

"Callous sod. You've a heart of stone, never to understand my pain."

"Never." Gavin turned away, for once his spirit not particularly uplifted by his friend's absurd banter.

Gavin couldn't blame Preshea. He'd known it was her nature to be cruel; he simply hadn't realized she was also petty. He wanted to know why. Why continue to goad poor Jack when he'd done himself over? Why bother? Why not a little compassion, if not for Jack, then for the sake of his friendship? She'd not given Gavin the chance to ask. He would have accepted any lie she offered, so as not to believe any worse of her character.

Instead, she had let him leave thinking ill of her. Not even tried. *She doesn't want me.* Gavin wallowed, too.

Preshea watched them depart. She hadn't slept. Her big Scotsman followed his friend out of Bickerstung Manor with those long, confident strides. His back was soldier-straight; a top hat hid his thick hair so she could not see what color it had decided to be this morning.

His face, when he realized what I'd done. Would he ever forgive her for humiliating a friend so? Likely not. *And I am too proud to ask. So, I've destroyed any chance I might have had to continue our liaison. Presuming I wished to.*

The carriage trundled away. They had elected, wisely, not to use the dirigible to return to the train station.

God, yes, I wish to. I never got to see what he could do kneeling before me while I stayed standing. We never tried other positions, other touches.

Certainly, this was nothing but lust. Lust driven by a profound curiosity and pursuit of a joy she'd never before known. She wanted Gavin because she feared she might never again know the sensations he incurred.

Unlikely that I would approach any other man. Preshea hated to admit why, even to herself. But she was ruthless with internal truth. One had to be if one's outer life was all lies. *Another man would not be*

Gavin. Would not understand how much I need quiet stillness. Would not have big hands, gentle and undemanding. My mountain of a Scotsman with a tongue that is only wicked without words.

You're pathetic, Preshea Buss. Pull yourself together.

The house party concluded with no further excitement. The Fenians did not try again. More's the pity; she could have used a distraction. They saved their wrath, as it turned out, for a Hyde Park rally some weeks later.

Preshea traveled back to London with the rest of the party. The Snodgrove party was returning to town. Lady Flo was to come out this season. The Blingchesters also intended to present their niece. There was shopping to do.

Miss Pagril and Lady Flo surprised Preshea by insisting she share their train carriage. The Bicker-Harrows and Blingchesters took one first-class compartment. Preshea could not fit in with them, and the duke would be safe enough at speed. Thus her choice was to travel with Miss Leeton, Lord Lionel, and Lady Violet, or with the younger girls. She assented to Miss Pagril's demanding her company, as she couldn't tolerate the idea of Lady Violet's unhappy face the entire trip to London.

She had chosen wisely. The conversation was light and comfortable. While never mentioned overtly, the two young ladies were grateful to Preshea for keeping their secret. Any harsh words were apparently forgotten. She was forgiven all for having concocted the headache excuse.

Travel to London took several hours, their train being of the regional variety that stopped at every inconsequential town. The young ladies didn't seem to mind Preshea's company, so long as her barbs were dulled and mostly not directed at them. They even laughed a few times. Preshea, strangely exhausted, found it easier to be kind. For a change.

As they pulled into London, Miss Pagril clasped Preshea's hand. "Dear Lady Villentia, I do hope we will see you at some of the upcoming social events? I know we are not your typical acquaintance, but perhaps you will make an exception?"

"My dear child, it is I who am not appropriate society for you. You would do better not to know me when we meet in public. I will not take it amiss."

Lady Flo was crestfallen. "We could never do that to a friend!"

Preshea was startled. She had never really had a friend before. And here were two, choosing her. *Only out of desperation that I keep their secret, surely.*

"You needn't worry. I shan't tell anyone anything." *What benefit would I reap from wrecking the lives of these two young lovers? The world will be hard enough on them. Anything I add would only be needless cruelty. Unless, of course, I stay friendly, keep an eye on them, cut others down who mean them harm.*

I'm getting soft in my old age. But she liked the idea. It would be a challenge.

Miss Pagril still pressed her hand. "Oh, we know that now. You aren't morally opposed and you genuinely don't seem to care."

Preshea pursed her lips. That was true enough. "Nevertheless, association with me will do neither of you any good."

"But it already has. We've learned so much." Miss Pagril would not be moved.

"How to waltz," suggested Lady Flo.

"How to sneak about without being caught."

"Now, Miss Pagril, there is a great deal more than my one-sentence explanation regarding misuse of candlelight."

"So, you must teach us." Miss Pagril's eyes danced.

Preshea sighed. Were she a better person, she would be neatly trapped by such enthusiasm. Then again, Miss Pagril did have a certain aptitude, although she was a bit old to start training now. Preshea's former finishing school no longer existed. *It might be fun to teach someone what I know.*

"Oh, very well, invite me to tea sometime, Miss Pagril, if your aunt will allow it. We shall test your mettle and go from there."

When the young ladies departed the carriage at the station, they were smiling.

Preshea arranged to share a cab with the Snodgrove party and saw the duke safely ensconced in his townhouse. No guns were fired, although she was twitchy during the entire ride and kept a hand to the weight of her revolver just in case.

Making her final farewells on the stoop, Preshea

recognized a group of dandies cavorting on a street corner nearby. Lord Akeldama's vanguard. She nodded to them as she passed, now alone in the cab. They hooted in a boisterous manner. As they should.

Her own house felt lean and empty in a way it never had before. It was her fourth husband's town residence, fashionable thirty years before, when he was in his prime. She'd never bothered to update it, since she didn't host parties and was frequently away. She kept a minimal staff, daytime servants only, whom she paid well for their discretion and her privacy.

The parlourmaid opened the door without comment. She was a strapping young thing, imported from the country, as Preshea preferred ability over appearance. The maid brought up her bags while her housekeeper paid the driver.

Preshea's dinner was waiting and she sat down to eat alone.

"I've a cold roast set aside for your supper, milady. Will there be anything else?" The housekeeper was an elderly Irishwoman, bespectacled and mostly deaf, but picky about accounts (a trait Preshea valued almost as much as her deafness).

"No, thank you, and tell the others they may go. I should like to be by myself this evening."

And so she was.

An envelope was waiting on her bed. She turned it over in her hands. Inside, the file was exactly as she remembered, with all the papers there as promised. She'd no concern that someone had broken into her chambers. She never kept anything of value in her home, and she'd none of her servants trained as guards. Preshea had long since realized that if she kept little of worth around her, few came hunting.

She stood for a time holding her father's fate, weighing it thoughtfully. Then, decisive, she addressed it to the *Mooring Standard* and put it out for the parlourmaid to post first thing. She set another letter atop it, directed to an obscure house in a posh part of town, asking if she might call an hour after sundown.

Lord Akeldama received Preshea in his drawing room this time. He wore a black velvet swallowtail coat over a silver and black striped waistcoat with inordinately tight silver knee britches. His hair, long despite current fashion, was queued back. The outfit was more modern than the ones he usually affected. But then, she had long since noticed, he tended to dress with more restraint when he was meeting with her.

Perhaps he is attempting to encourage sympathy by reflecting my own style back at me?

"You've read today's *Standard*?" she asked without greeting.

"Indeed I have, *star* of the heavens. You look lovely tonight – I do adore you in red."

She did not require a compliment, so she did not acknowledge it. She was well aware that her crimson evening gown was heavenly; it had cost the moon, after all.

"So, we are done now?" Her tone was not kind.

The vampire rolled his eyes at her abruptness. "The duke, as I understand it, is safely back in London. The situation with his daughter satisfactorily settled. I must own to some surprise that you felt the need to visit me at all. Surely, you know the matter was settled the moment you returned to town with him still alive."

"It was an easy assignment. You will not require my services again? I have a feeling the Second Reform Act will pass."

"Even I cannot control the masses. But yes, we are done. I shall miss you, my *sparkling ruby*."

"You have always enjoyed collecting pretty things."

He inclined his head. "The time may come again when I have something you want, and you can do something I need."

Preshea puffed out her cheeks. "And if I wish to retire?"

The vampire blinked. For the first time in their association, he looked genuinely startled. "How peculiar. Do you think that likely? You are not so old, my jewel. Or *are* you? I lose track of mortal time so easily."

The old fangs wasn't pulling one over on Preshea. No doubt he knew her age, likely to the month.

Preshea didn't trust Lord Akeldama. She recognized a fellow predator, and she recognized that this one could best her. She did not like to be in the inferior position. But she did respect him.

Suddenly, she burned with a need to ask him to explain everything: the working of men's hearts (or at least that of one Scotsman) and her own confused feelings. Why had he left her, and why had she allowed it?

The vampire would know. He had everything. All the wealth he needed, any information he craved, avenues of manipulation, and immeasurable power. And he had time to use it, all the time in the world.

"Lord Akeldama, may I ask you an impertinent question?"

"Gracious, my diamond girl. How exciting. I *adore* impertinent questions. Ask away!"

"What would you do, if you were I and had only the one life to live?"

"As if I should remember what it was like to be mortal? Preposterous. You *know* what I did. I chose not to live it at all. I chose to step outside of time." For one shocking moment, a slight twitch of his eyelid, and Preshea thought he might regret that choice. *A vampire, regret immortality? Surely not.*

"I find myself at an impasse." She decided to explain a little. In case he really didn't understand her plight. "I've served my indenture, relatively untroubled. Thank you for that. I've gained through the experience modest wealth and standing. I've no need to ply the trade for which I was trained, although I am good at it. The days stretch out before me with little to occupy them."

"Go shopping," he said promptly.

"Yes, I was considering Paris." A dig there, at a man who was trapped forever within a mile or so radius of his London home.

"Touché." He followed her exactly. "Travel, then, star of the night. Travel."

"Is that what you would do?"

"It's what I did. I was a great traveler before I grew my fangs. Trotted over most of the known world. Of course, it wasn't as big back then." He gave one of those tight vampire smiles, showing no teeth, meaning no insult.

"And was that enough?" Preshea wasn't certain what she wanted out of this conversation. Actually, she was, but wasn't sure why it had to be Lord Akeldama. *I want him to tell me to go to Gavin. Why is it an ancient vampire with a predilection for spying whose judgment I need? What is Lord Akeldama to me? An old master. An old monster. Certainly not a friend. Why do I require him to tell me what I already know?*

Because he is old. Because if he tells me to do it, it's as close as I may come to the wisdom of the ages. Because he has made the same choice a thousand times. I have seen him do it. I only need to know if it was also right when he was mortal.

The vampire was frowning – eyes serious, unblemished forehead creased only slightly. "What do you need me to say, little jewel? I am one for riddles as a general rule, but I do not like to be confused by mortal *waffling*."

"Did you love them all? I mean *really* love them?"

"My darling drones?"

"Yes."

"Every single one."

"And before there were drones. When you were traveling the known world. Did you love him?" For there must have been a him, even then. Not matter how long ago *then* was.

He froze; all light and feeling fled his face, leaving him truly corpselike. Which he was, of course – only, normally Lord Akeldama didn't actually look it.

"Very much." His gaze focused on some ghost no one else would ever see and no one but he remembered.

"And would you do that again, if you had the chance?"

"Without question." He looked pained, but in the way of vampires. For all his hurt was so long ago and so desiccated by history that it had become bloodless – aching, no doubt, but bloodless.

His focus returned to her, and in one of those lightning movements, almost too fast for the human eye to follow, he was sitting next to her on the settee, her small hand in his cold one.

"Listen to me, my deadly little pearl. Choose love. *Always* choose love. If the decision is between love and anything else, choose love."

"And if he hurts me?"

"It is worth it."

"And if I hurt him?"

"My dear, you know hundreds of ways to kill a man. Simply ensure that you put him out of his misery quickly."

Preshea did not ask him to be serious; Lord

Akeldama had clearly used up all his seriousness for one evening. She was lucky to have gotten even that much out of him. Also, she understood what he was really saying. It was Gavin's right to take the risk of being hurt, just as it was hers.

So, I will see if he would like the opportunity.

Gavin returned home after a night of unsatisfactory cards and disappointing company. Mawkins dismissed, he turned towards his bed.

There she sat, cross-legged, as if she had always been there. She was wearing some diaphanous garment that made her look part angel, part seductress.

"Holy hell, lass, where in God's name did you spring from!" He sloshed his glass of claret.

"Language."

"You truly are some mythic creature."

She only smiled. "Come to bed, Gavin."

"Am I dreaming? I must be dreaming."

She patted the pillow next to her, waiting.

"How did you find me?"

She shook her head a tiny bit at him, raising her eyebrows. "You do remember what I do for work, don't you?"

Gavin decided perhaps he would not open his mouth again until he had his brain in order. So, he stripped – he'd been about to do that anyway. He set aside the claret. He'd found, since returning to London, that he needed the wine more than before.

Now his ghosts were more often Preshea-shaped than not, and they visited more frequently. And yet there she sat, apparently in the flesh.

He climbed in under the covers, as though she weren't there.

She unfolded and snuggled down under the blankets too, turning to face him, propping her cheek on one hand. She stared at him from only a few inches away.

"Scruffy. You didn't shave this evening?"

"I dinna know you were coming. You dinna send word." *She still smells of peaches.*

"I wanted to surprise you."

"Consider me surprised. And bearded."

"I'm sorry."

"So you should be. Beards are fair inconvenient when combined with my preferred pastime. I assume that's what you're here about?"

"Not about that."

He stopped ribbing her in favor of real answers. "It's been three weeks, lass! How could you let me go like that?" He let her feel his hurt. He'd thought her gone forever, but he'd remained in London. *London! During the season!* He'd stayed in a place he hated on the slim chance that she would come looking. And now he was profoundly, bone-meltingly relieved that she had. Not to mention angry that it had taken her so long. And –

"I'm sorry about Mr Jackson."

"Jack? What does *Jack* have to do with it?"

"I set him up – the dirigible and the piccolo. It was a contract, too. I was there for both. Jack at the duke's behest, and the duke at—"

"Na the werewolves. They dinna know you'd been set to watch like me."

"You were there for them?"

He nodded.

She gave back in kind. "I was there for the vampires. Jack was a necessary casualty. I hope he wasn't too hurt?"

"Hang Jack! He's a woolen-headed dolt. He's already gone and fallen in love again. Some American heiress."

Preshea laughed. "So, you're angry I let you leave without saying anything? What did you want me to say?"

She ran a fingertip around his jaw, as if testing the scratch of his nightly beard. It would scrape her thighs. *Weel, she deserves it. I'll find a nice cooling cloth for after, make certain she doesna get too red... What am I thinking? She left me in misery for weeks and here I'm worrying about her thighs. Of course I am.* Gavin sighed; he wasn't even angry with her. *Because she is here, with me.*

He answered her question. "I wanted you to ask me to stay. Even though I couldna. I wanted you to offer to continue our liaison."

"Only that?"

I wanted you to say you loved me. But there was no way he was going to scare her off with that.

"Lass, I read about your father, in the papers."

"How did you know he's my father?"

"Preshea *Buss.*" She winced and he hurried on. "I called in my favor with the werewolves of the War

Office soon as I returned. They've a wee file on you, verra wee. Had all your names, though. Weel, all the public ones. Was it your doing, then, 'the humiliation of Mr Buss'?" He quoted the headline.

"Quite the scandal. He's fled to Australia, did you know? Won't ever be able to practice business here again." He'd sold shoddy materials to a dirigible manufacturer. People had died when the airship exploded. Lord Akeldama had acquired the company articles, and Preshea's father was culpable without question.

"Are you tainted by association, lass?"

She shrugged, still caressing his face. "Not hardly. It's been years since I carried his name. We never appeared in public together."

"You're staying in London, then?" He was disappointed. If she were escaping scandal, she might wish to come with him back to the rolling, endless green of his beloved Scotland.

She grinned, a real smile that crept all the way into those remarkable eyes. "Actually, I believe I should like to travel."

"The season has only just begun."

"Second Reform Act has people restless. There could be riots. I've no need to stay in town."

"Season would give you the opportunity to catch another husband. You're out of mourning."

"What would I do with another husband?"

"You might pick one you actually loved for a change."

"You applying for the position?"

Startled, Gavin reached for her hand and held it

between his, stopping the caresses.

"Am I in with a chance?"

She broke the moment. At least, he *thought* that was what she was doing. "I had an interesting conversation with a vampire recently."

"Oh, aye?"

"He said something very wise."

"Vampires are known to do that, on occasion."

"He said I should choose love."

Gavin stopped breathing. He could do nothing but stare at her – small white face, slight up-tilt to the nose, bluest of blue eyes, all polished perfection. "Did he, now?"

"Although I'm sure he wouldn't approve of the beard."

Gavin sat up and yelled, "Mawkins! Get your scrawny arse in here!"

Preshea hit him with a tiny fist. "Don't be an idiot!"

The valet's head appeared around the door. "Sir?" He didn't even blink at Preshea's presence. She hid under the coverlet. Gavin was given to wonder if Mawkins hadn't a hand in letting her into the room in the first place. *Crafty devil.*

"My lass here would see me shaved."

"Now, sir?"

Preshea's head popped back up. She pressed her mouth against Gavin's ear. In front of his valet! Gavin blushed a little, although the situation was entirely of his own making.

She whispered, "We can test out the beard. Perhaps if I am standing, it will not prickle quite so much?"

"Thank you, Mawkins, that will be all."

"Sir." Mawkins left promptly. He was grinning like a madman.

Gavin lifted her and rolled so she rested atop him. Her full length pressed along his. "Love, is it?"

"Aye." She mocked his accent and then added, "And?" Her voice almost trembled.

He could have teased her more, but he never would be the kind of man to let a lady suffer. Especially not this one. "Silly lass. 'Course I love you. Wouldna dare not to." He liked knowing she could kill him. There was probably something wrong with that, but since her ability wasn't going away, he'd rather enjoy it than not. He didn't tell her, though. A surprise for later.

"I've given over assassinations for the time being."

"Suit yourself." He began shifting her up his body, licking down to her breasts and stomach. *She tastes like peaches, too.*

"Although I might have agreed to train a friend. We will have to return to London occasionally."

"If we must." He delved lower, and her voice stuttered as her breathing altered. Then he realized what she'd just said. He lifted her back down to sit on his chest. "Train? Train who?"

"Miss Pagril."

"What!"

"She'll need it more than most."

"She's only a wee lass."

"Exactly."

"Weel." He paused to consider. He supposed it wouldn't be such a bad thing if the young miss had some skill in sneaking about. "I see your point. But could we leave Miss Pagril out of matters for the moment?" His tone was plaintive.

She laughed, wriggled off him, and jumped out of bed, pulling the long, filmy gown over her head.

"Come along, then. I believe there was mention of testing the efficaciousness of kneeling, beards, and tongues."

She was perfect, and she was waiting for him. So, Gavin went and knelt, presenting the beard and the tongue in equal measure for her assessment.

Preshea was very exacting, and she did get prickled. Later, much later, he did go find a cooling cloth. At which point she said sleepily that she didn't mind. And wondered if she would like Scotland.

Gavin told her she would love it. For Scotland, being both ruthless and beautiful, appreciated both in others.

She gave a tiny sigh and curled against him. "I do love you. It's a most peculiar sensation. Not unlike the beard. A great deal of pleasure is to be had, but I know it will likely hurt in the end."

"Look at it from my perspective," he teased.

"I did. That's why I stayed away so long. Then I decided it was unfair. I wasn't allowing you your choice."

"Wise lass. I intend to be particularly good at loving you."

And he was.

And Preshea learned to be quite good at loving

him, in due time.

And Gavin never again forgot to shave of an evening.

AUTHOR'S NOTE

Thank you so much for picking up *Poison or Protect*. If you enjoyed this story, please consider leaving a review. I'm grateful for the time you take to do so.

I have a silly gossipy newsletter called the Monthly Chirrup. I promise: no spam, no fowl. (Well, maybe a little fowl.)

If you'd like to know when my next book releases, that newsletter is best. If you are not inclined to chirrup, I've a fun website with links to my Twitter and a fan discussion group on Facebook.

Thank you!

www.GailCarriger.com

ABOUT THE AUTHOR

New York Times bestselling author Gail Carriger writes to cope with being raised in obscurity by an expatriate Brit and an incurable curmudgeon. She escaped small-town life and inadvertently acquired several degrees in higher learning, a fondness for cephalopods, and a chronic tea habit. She then traveled the historic cities of Europe, subsisting entirely on biscuits secreted in her handbag. She resides in the Colonies, surrounded by fantastic shoes, where she insists on tea imported from London.

www.GailCarriger.com

Lightning Source UK Ltd.
Milton Keynes UK
UKOW03f0808120417
298943UK00003B/64/P